BACKLESS, STRAPLESS & SLIT TO THE THROAT

A FEMME FATALE ANTHOLOGY

Edited by Betty Dobson

InkSpotter Publishing

BACKLESS, STRAPLESS & SLIT TO THE THROAT

A FEMME FATALE ANTHOLOGY

PUBLISHED BY INKSPOTTER PUBLISHING
163 Main Avenue, Halifax, Nova Scotia, Canada B3M 1B3
http://inkspotter.com/

Copyright © 2008 InkSpotter Publishing

Printed and bound in the United States of America by CreateSpace

Library and Archives Canada Cataloguing in Publication

Backless, strapless & slit to the throat : a femme fatale anthology / edited by Betty Dobson.

Includes index.
ISBN 978-0-9739896-2-5

1. Femmes fatales—Literary collections. 2. Femmes fatales—Fiction. 3. Short stories, American. 4. Short stories, Canadian (English). 5. American fiction—21st century. 6. Canadian fiction (English)—21st century. I. Dobson, Betty, 1962- II. Title: Backless, strapless and slit to the throat.
PS648.W6B34 2008 813'.087208 C2008-907389-4

CONTENTS

ACKNOWLEDGEMENTS

"The Right Man" was originally published in *Fedora III* (Wildside Press, 2004).

"Simply Irresistible" was originally published by Donard Publishing (www.donardpublishing.com) as the winner of their May 2003 Short Story Competition.

OLE FRED AND A MEXICAN MARSALIS
Gary R. Hoffman

Damned Tony Marsalis! I have never seen him in any tavern except Smitty's, and now I walk into The Brown Bear, and there he is sitting at the bar. Now granted, I don't frequent too many bars except Smitty's myself, but I do get around a few others in my work. My name is Meg Bartlett, and I've been a private detective for a little over eight years now in St. Louis.

I've kind of had a thing for Marsalis for several years now. The worst part was that tonight I was wearing my Super Slut outfit, attempting to see if some guy would try to pick me up. His wife had hired me to see if he was cheating on her. I was going to give him the chance.

Super Slut was one of my own little characters. I wore more makeup than usual, fishnet stockings, a short skirt and low cut blouse. A small part of my lacy red bra did a peek-a-boo number right at the vee of the blouse. I added a lot of bling with cheap rhinestone jewellery. So here I was standing in front of the last person on earth I wanted to view me as a slut and looking more like a slut than most sluts do!

Tony glanced at me and then did a double take. He set his beer on the bar and spun around on his stool. He got a big grin on his face. "Well, well. Look at you. This how you spend your free time?"

I grabbed the stool next to him. "Not hardly. I'm working," I said, trying to keep my voice down.

He snickered and looked sideways at me. "At what?"

I elbowed him in the arm. "I came in here trying to see if some guy would try to pick me up." He snickered again. "A guy I'm following!" Another snicker. "For a client! She wants to see if he's cheating on her."

He leaned back and eyed me up and down. I have to admit a crazy chill ran down my spine and settled in an area he knew all too well—and could do marvellous things with! "Isn't there such a thing as entrapment?"

It was then I saw Robert Kyle. He was sitting in a booth talking with a woman. I got out my cell phone and pretended to make a call. They were showing up real good on the mirror in front of me, so I got their pictures by looking straight ahead. Within five minutes, they left the bar together. I got some more pictures. I now knew this was my lucky day—I had pictures of the guy I wanted and was with Marsalis! "Want to go to your place or mine?" I asked him.

"You want me to leave this bar with a woman who looks like you do? I do have a reputation to uphold."

My turn to snicker. "Your reputation died when you were two days old and tried to pat a nurse on the ass!"

He took the last swallow of his beer. "Your place. Mine's a disaster area!"

While driving to my apartment, I called Mrs. Kyle and told her what I had. She wanted to meet with me the next morning. Since she had money for me, I agreed, even though I knew it was going to be an effort on my part. Much later that night or maybe early the next morning, while on the downhill side of a fantastic situation, I mumbled something to Tony about making sure I was awake before he left for work.

What happened next seemed to happen very close to the time I told him that. He threw the blankets back, drug my naked body into the shower, turned on the cold water, and left for work. It was actually several hours later, but in my state of blissful fatigue, it seemed much shorter. There was only one good thing about it—it got me to my appointment on time, something which doesn't always happen after a night of Marsalis. I was to meet with Mrs. Kyle at Smitty's for a cup of coffee at nine, and I was there ten minutes early. I was proud of myself.

The thing I wasn't proud of was my choice of underwear for the day. In my haste to get dressed, I picked out a pair of panties that I usually reserve for those days when everything else is in the dirty clothes. They were now riding very low—and heading further south with each step I took. I was thankful I had worn jeans so they would stop when they got to the crotch.

Mrs. Kyle didn't show! This was maddening on any morning, but on this morning, it ranked a fifteen on a scale of one to ten. I knew from trailing her husband he should be at work, so I headed over to her house. My car payment was due in two days. By the time I got to her front door, I was in no mood to use a doorbell. I pounded on the door. It swung open. Things like this were always a bad omen for me, and this one didn't disappoint me. I found her body in a pool of blood on the kitchen floor. I clicked a picture of her with my cell phone before I called the police. Maybe Sol Rothschild, the guy who sold me the car and financed it, would have some compassion for me if he saw a picture of the woman who was supposed to provide the payment. I really had doubts about that because when I was close with a payment, I had to go see Sol in person. He spent most of our time together talking to my chest. I looked at the woman lying on the floor again. Blood isn't my favourite thing, so I went outside to call the police.

Fortunately, one of the law enforcement people who showed up was Detective Mel Short. Mel and I had worked together on several cases, and he was a good friend with my dad who had been a beat cop for over twenty years. Mel had his new partner with him, Linda Sovereign.

"So where does the husband work?" Mel asked after I explained how I was involved in all this.

"Delbert Tandy Investments. His wife told me he was some kind of a broker there."

"Got an address?"

As soon as he had the address, he called for a couple of squad cars to bring Robert Kyle into the station. Forensics people were now starting to swarm the place. We went to the front porch to finish our conversation.

"You got the pictures with you that you were going to give her?" Mel asked.

"Sure."

He glanced over them. "Any idea who the woman is?"

"None."

"How long you been following him?"

"Three days. Yesterday was the first time I actually got anything on him."

"And that was at The Brown Bear?"

"Yep."

"Okay. Take off now. I'll be in touch if I need anything else." I left, being very careful how I walked. My panties were in a precarious position at the time. I headed for Smitty's. My stomach was growling.

The "anything else" came the next afternoon. Mel called me as I was thinking about trying to clean up my office. Saved by the bell again!

"First," he started, "we found a check written out to you in Mrs. Kyle's purse. I'm not supposed to do this, but I'm going to give it to you. We've got a copy of it."

"Great! I can stay in my apartment for another month!"

"Second, when you got there, did you see anyone else close to the house? Even someone walking down the sidewalk?"

"Not that I remember. Why?"

"Coroner says she was only dead a few minutes when you got there, if I've got my timeline right. The killer could have still been in the neighbourhood or even in the house. We've canvassed everyone in the neighbourhood. Nobody saw anything unusual."

"Wish I could say yes, but I didn't see anyone else. How about the husband?"

"Got an alibi tighter than last year's blue jeans. He was in a meeting with five other people."

"Could he have hired it done?"

"Possible. He got some bonus cheques that never made the joint bank account. He does admit to cheating on his wife and says that's where the extra money went."

"Your forensics people turn up anything?"

"Only that she was stabbed with a butcher knife from her own kitchen. A weapon of convenience. She did have some broken fingernails on her right hand and a bruise on her left hand. Maybe trying to fight off whoever did this."

That night, I got a call from Robert Kyle. He wanted to hire me to find his wife's killer. I told him the police could do a better job than I could, but he insisted on shoving money in my direction, so I took it. He figured the more people working on the case the better chance someone would find the killer. I figured this could be just a way of setting up a smoke screen—he wanted to make himself look innocent. Either way, I took the job.

The next day, I went back to see Mel, explained what I was doing, and asked to see all the evidence he had so far. His new partner wasn't thrilled about the idea, but Mel came through for me. I sat for a long time studying the photos of Mrs. Kyle. I couldn't put my finger on anything, but something didn't seem right to me. I got out my cell phone and started flipping through the pictures I had stored in it. When I found the picture I had taken of Mrs. Kyle, I sheepishly explained to Mel why I had taken it.

"But look at this. This is different from the ones your people took. Look at her left hand in my picture. It is clenched tight and something is sticking out from the side of her fist. Looks like a white piece of cloth. Look at your pictures. The hand is open. Nothing is in it."

Mel compared both pictures. "And you said you went out on the porch to call the police?"

"Yes."

"You know what that means?"

I got another cold chill, and not a Marsalis' one. "Yeah. The killer was probably still in the house when I first came in. They left when I went out to call you guys."

"That would be my guess," Linda finally chimed in.

"Then someone should have seen them," Mel said. "It's a pretty quiet neighbourhood. Surely someone would have noticed a stranger there."

"Unless they weren't a stranger," I told them.

Early the next morning, I was back in the Kyles' neighbourhood. It appeared many of the people there left for work between seven and eight, and that most couples both left. A painter came in to work on one house. Lawn care services started showing up. Package delivery trucks came into the area. It then dawned on me why no one saw any strangers in the area. It was someone who would normally be there. Like one of these service people. These are called invisible people. They show up all the time, but no one really notices them.

I saw a man next door pulling some weeds from around his shrubbery. "Morning."

He was rather startled, but answered. "Good morning. Can I help you?"

I showed him my PI badge. "Were you home the other day when Mrs. Kyle was killed?"

"Yes. That was tragic, wasn't it? And scary. You know you see that sort of thing on the news, but you never expect it to happen here. And right next door!"

"Yeah, I can understand that. I just wanted to ask you a couple of questions."

"Well, I told the other policeman all I knew."

I smiled at him. "Maybe he just didn't ask the right questions. I'm interested in anyone you may have seen in the area that didn't belong here."

"Well, they asked that question, and I had to tell them no. Wish I had seen someone. Maybe that would help."

"You remember any package delivery vans being in the neighbourhood that day?"

"Sure. One of them is here almost every day. Can't say which one was here that day, though. Like I said, there's lots of them."

"Anybody working on lawns around close?"

"Again, almost every day. Bob did hire a company to do his lawn, but they weren't here that day."

"Is there anybody, anybody at all who may be in the

service business you can remember being around that day?"

"Come to think of it, there was one . . . No, they aren't really in the service business."

"And who might that have been, sir?"

"Well, the guy who reads electric meters came that day. Come to think of it, he was a couple days early."

"Did he read your meter?"

"I really don't know. I saw him over in the Kyles' backyard. I went in for a drink of water and when I came back out, he was gone. I didn't see him anywhere down the block either."

"Would you have seen him if he read your meter?"

"Probably. It's out by our back door, and I left the door open." He put his hands up to his mouth. "Oh, good heavens! If that was the killer he could have just walked in on us, too."

"Well, I don't think he was after you, sir. Was it the regular guy who reads meters in this neighbourhood or someone different?"

"Oh, it was Fred. He's been reading meters around here for two or three years."

"I appreciate the information. Thanks for your time."

"When you're retired, you have a lot of that."

I called Mel as soon as I got back to my car. I knew he had the clout to find out more about ole Fred than I did.

The information got to me quicker than I figured it would. I was at Smitty's the next morning eating breakfast after I discovered my fridge was bare. I vowed to go to the grocery store as soon as I finished breakfast. Like most people, I knew better than to go grocery shopping on an empty stomach.

I was at my usual back booth when Mel came in. He got a cup of coffee and joined me. "Well, this one turned out to be easier than I thought it would," he said.

"The husband hired the meter reader, right?"

"Sorry. We picked up Fred McNally. At first, he knew nothing. Then we discovered the electric company requires their meter readers to wear uniforms, but the readers are responsible for their own uniforms. Fred had just ordered a new shirt. We found his old one in the trash at his house. The pocket flap was torn off. Not only that, but there was Mrs. Kyle's blood on it."

"So why did he do it?"

"Did Mrs. Kyle tell you anything about why she wanted information about her husband cheating?"

"Yeah, she was going to divorce him. Wanted more ammo when she went to court."

"And in many of these cases, why does the woman want a divorce?" he asked me.

"What the hell is this—twenty questions?"

"Just think about it."

I thought, which was not my best feature early in the morning. "Because she has a boyfriend on the side?"

"Bingo! And who was the boyfriend?"

"Ole Fred!"

"And?"

"She wanted a divorce to marry Fred, but he didn't want to divorce his wife. They got into an argument, and he stabbed her."

"Hey, you not only win the money, but a trip to Mexico!"

"Don't I wish." I paused. "If I go to Mexico, can I take someone with me?"

Mel smiled. "Dream on!"

I did, which is one of my better features all the time. I wondered what a Mexican Marsalis would be like.

VELVET GARDENS
Brenda Roberts

Long brown hair veils
Eyes—hazel and velvet brown
with passion.

Roses bloom
on cheeks full of life
and joy.

Tulips of scarlet red
open in a smile of
love and laughter.

Tendrils of softest
rose-moss caress
the gardener's face

as finger-trowels
open furrows of
fragrant earth

ready for planting
new seeds of trust
to grow in a velvet garden

as Spring, pregnant with
tomorrow, bursts forth in
orgasmic glory.

AWAITING HER

Gail A. Laursen

Awaiting her
With candles glowing—
Their golden spheres
Dancing with shadows
That weave dark things
From his precious love.

Another gust of wind roared over the small Cape Cod home, hammering it with pelting rain. Dorian pulled his face back from the onslaught at the window, repositioned himself before continuing his vigil.

He strained to see beyond the azaleas and laurel hedges that they'd planted when he and Kara first moved in—they hid the drive now. He fixed his gaze instead on the one visible stretch of winding coast highway which glistened in the rainy darkness.

"Where *are* you, Kara?" Dorian worried aloud.

She was always late. Dorian knew that. *So why should tonight be any different?* he reproached himself. Yet his thoughts still led him places he didn't want to go, conjured images he didn't want to see.

A heavy torrent blasted the window. Dorian's view blurred. He turned away just as soft chimes played the first measure of "Big Ben."

The antique clock Kara had bought on a whim loomed into Dorian's view. Three-fifteen . . . tick-tick-tick . . . it was merciless.

Dorian roused himself from the bay window's bench and paced the floor, his fears and suspicions dogging every step, threatening to overwhelm him.

Then, the lights flickered and went out.

"No! Not now!" Kara pushed away from Rodney and groped her way to the window. She yanked the curtain back and inventoried the scene. "Great! The whole town is blacked out."

"So what?" Rodney reached out and drew her to him. "What does it matter?"

Kara sat down on the bed beside him. She fussed, straightening her jacket and adjusting her blouse.

"C'mon, Sugar." Rodney stroked Kara's arm. "I need more . . . ahem, collateral for *this* job."

"What?" Kara drew away, shooting off an icy glare.

Rodney froze.

"You promised!" A frown creased Kara's forehead.

"I know. I will!" Rodney slid up against her, breathing hot expectations on the nape of her neck. "Just once more for good faith. How 'bout it?"

Kara shivered and stood up. Lifting a mirror from her purse, she said, "I've got to go. It's late." She squinted at the mirror and tousled her blonde locks by the ghostly light eking through the window.

"Whatever . . . uh . . . what'd you say your name is?"

"Never mind—" Kara M-ed her lips briefly before smiling seductively. "—you don't need it."

"But I thought . . . you and me . . ."

"Now, there's the problem." Kara added with a saucy wink. "I didn't pick you for your brains."

Rodney puzzled for an instant then, with a lascivious grin, grabbed for her again.

Kara side-stepped his grasp. "No. I can't. Not now." Her eyes flashed another chilly warning. "I've got to do this *tonight!*" She began pacing restlessly.

Rodney watched, bemused, as Kara tread an erratic path across the motel room floor. When she finally stopped, he searched her shadowed face for the frightened woman who had picked him up—a soaked hitch-hiker with a flat tire—off the highway hours ago. Perhaps it was only her need for his help that made her warm so quickly to Rodney's charms, but he didn't care. Rodney smirked recalling their passion.

Kara's voice cut sharply into his reverie. "If you don't want to help me, just say so!"

"I never said nothin' about backing out." Rodney stood suddenly and, thumping his chest with his palm, said proudly, "I'm a man of my word!"

Kara pulled the curtain back further and pointed out the window. "Yeah, well, how are you going to protect me if you can't even see him?" Her rant spent, she turned away, shoulders quivering ever so slightly.

"Now, c'mon." Rodney rushed over to her and, drawing her close, cooed hoarsely, "Don't cry. I won't let that jerk hurt one hair on your pretty little head!"

Kara sniffed and folded herself into Rodney's embrace. "You promise?"

Dorian lit the last pillar candle and placed it atop the large wooden holder near the door. *Some light for Kara,* he thought before returning to his post at the bay window.

The deluge continued. Though as the night sky paled the sodden shroud was lifting. The view of the highway was getting better.

If only I hadn't pushed her! Dorian's mental tortures continued. *Everything was going so much better! Why did I have to bring up children again?* He shook his head.

Without warning, the image of Kara atop Greg, his then-business-partner, scorched its way across his mind's eye. Dorian winced and clenched the cushion. Kara's other flings had never hurt so badly.

But that was five years ago and they'd made great progress since then. Or so the therapist assured him. *Kara seems happier,* Dorian reassured himself. *She might even get to like domestic life,* he mused hopefully. Her forays into the club district had definitely slowed. Though that's where she probably went after he'd brought up "that subject" again tonight.

The clock chimed out the full refrain of "Big Ben" and readied itself, with a subtle whirr, to stoically clang four bells. Ding-ding-ding-ding.

Dorian stared at the contraption, loathing it.

"There." Rodney pointed to the black Harley propped against a tree, its rear hub resting on a block of wood.

Kara pulled in beside the bike and stopped. Rodney jumped out, signalling for Kara to pop the trunk, and was soon loping, wheel in hand, toward his bike.

Kara watched as Rodney began working. His Def Leppard t-shirt, soaked again already, clung deliciously to his body. She smirked, recalling her recent conquest.

As Rodney manoeuvred the wheel into place Kara began probing his backpack. Soon, she felt the cold of the gun's walnut grip seeping through her lambskin gloves. She withdrew the revolver he had shown her earlier, opened the cylinder, and checked the ammo.

Two bullets would have to do.

Rodney yanked the wrench. His hand slipped, knuckles smashing the gravel below. Cussing and shaking his injured hand, he grimaced at the rain blurred image of Kara inside her Lexus.

Kara grinned and waved as her other hand carefully placed the gun inside her purse. Then she reached over, turned on the radio, and waited, tapping the steering wheel in time with the music.

Elton John's "The Bitch is Back" throbbed fuzzily at Rodney as he stowed his tire iron.

The house looked dark from the highway. But after parking the car, Kara noticed the glow of candlelight emanating from the bay window. She fumed and ran for the porch as a motorbike thundered by on the highway, its sound soon lost in the drizzle and fog.

"Thank God!" Dorian said when she burst through the front door. He rushed to hug her.

"Dori, stop." Kara raised a manicured hand. "I just came home to get some things. I'll get the rest later."

"But—"

"But nothing! There's nothing to talk about!" Kara pushed past him. "How many times have we been over this?"

"No, Kara! Don't do this!" Dorian reached out, grabbed her arm, and spun her to face him.

Suddenly the front door banged open behind him. Kara's eyes grew wide.

"Keep your filthy hands off her!" a male voice boomed.

Dorian swung around to see—briefly, before losing consciousness—a ham-sized fist looming from a muscle-extruding Def Leppard t-shirt.

"Don't move," the nurse ordered Dorian. Into the phone's receiver she said, "Mr. Hale is awake, Doctor." She replaced the receiver and explained, "Dr. Thomas will be right with you."

"What's going on? Where's my wife?" Dorian's parched mouth fumbled his words. Only his mind raced.

The nurse gave him a sympathetic look while checking his pulse, but gave no answer.

Within minutes, the Sheriff arrived with his deputy and the doctor. Dorian looked at them with foreboding. "Wh . . . what's happened?" He tried to sit up but his head felt as though it would split. "Where's Kara?" Wincing, Dorian held his bandaged head and lay back.

"What do you remember, Mr. Hale?" The sheriff nodded to his deputy who stood nearby, ready to take notes.

Dorian frowned. It hurt. He closed his eyes, exhaling his pain. "N . . . nothing much. A fist, a t-shirt, that's about all."

"I'm sorry to tell you this, Mr. Hale, but your wife is dead." The sheriff watched Dorian's face closely as he delivered his news.

"What?" Dorian's eyes flew open, and he sprang up in bed. Groaning, he grabbed his head with both hands and reeled.

"That's enough!" the doctor chided the sheriff as he helped Dorian settle back. "This man has a serious concussion."

Dorian croaked, "The light . . ." and the nurse obediently closed the drapes and dimmed the lights before leaving. "How . . . ?" A cry broke from Dorian, and he began weeping. That hurt even more.

The sheriff and doctor exchanged looks. The doctor nodded.

"Your wife was murdered, Mr. Hale." The sheriff watched Dorian intently. "It appears the intruder who beat you also beat your wife. She was pronounced dead at the scene."

Dorian's eyes grew wide. "No!" Tears spilled over his eyelids and tracked down his cheek. "What . . . I mean . . . how . . . ?"

Again the sheriff and doctor exchanged glances. "Your wife died from severe blunt force trauma to the head. But she may have shot her assailant before she was killed. We found gunshot residue on your wife's hand. The gun hasn't been found yet."

Dorian shook his head, struggling to absorb the news.

"Odd thing . . ." The sheriff paused, waiting for Dorian to look up. "There was no blood trace. And your assailant took the gun but never used it. He also took the blunt instrument he used on your skulls." Holding Dorian's gaze, the sheriff added, "Do you know of any reason why someone would want to harm you or your wife?

Dorian was stunned. "N . . . no. Why would anyone want to hurt *us*?"

The sheriff studied Dorian's red-rimmed eyes. Then he nodded to his deputy, who closed his notepad and stepped over to the door. "We'll leave you now. Get some rest, Mr. Hale. I'll send Deputy Rowlands back tomorrow to take a formal statement."

When Dorian was released from hospital a week later, he told the realty agent who brokered the house he couldn't return home where Kara's murder would haunt him. The local motel became his new home.

It quickly became obvious Kara's death had driven him to despair. In mad purges, Dorian posted ads and held garage sales—even an auction—in a relentless effort to sell off their belongings. A month later he sold the Lexus. Everything, he insisted, reminded him of Kara.

But it wasn't until Dorian used the proceeds from the sale of the house to buy a brand new Harley Davidson that any shred of understanding his friends had remaining was irrevocably torn. No one was surprised when Dorian said he was moving away.

Dorian revved his blood-red Harley, enjoying the growl beneath him, and called down to Rodney. "It's good to be back in the saddle, ol' buddy!"

Rodney tossed a large wooden candlestick, wrapped in a black t-shirt and chain, out into the ocean. Next, the revolver was launched, soaring farther out over the drop-off before plunking into the depths. Turning back and climbing the rocky embankment, he answered, "I thought you liked all that domestic crap."

"I did." Dorian shook his head and added, "If only Kara had."

Rodney nodded glumly and glanced up at his friend.

Dorian returned his look. Their eyes remained locked until Dorian looked away, back down the coast highway, and said, "When I dropped you off with the flat that night, I wasn't sure if—"

Rodney cut him off sharply. "She was a creature of habit, man!"

"I know. I know. I just hoped . . ."

Rod straddled the guard rail and paused. "Hey, she would've busted your unconscious head open with that candlestick if I hadn't stopped her."

"Yeah, I know." Dorian rubbed his scar thoughtfully. "Thanks, Rod."

"We're even, man." Rodney mounted his bike. "If I hadn't loaded blanks like you told me to, that witch would've killed me, too!"

Dorian nodded reluctant agreement. Then, without another word, they donned helmets, put the Harleys in gear, and rumbled away into the dawn.

FINGERNAILS

Everett C. Gavel, Jr.

You peel back my fingernails
Slow, methodical
Bit by bit, each day anew
Ripping them from the skin

Searing pain floods my world
In red-tinted water
You laugh as I cry
My screams ignored,

A tear hits my raw flesh
Where a jagged nail once nested
Shudders and anguish overwhelm
Kicked in the head by laughter

Our life is such,
Now that you have let him in.

FIFTY BUCKS
Betty Dobson

Maggie pulled her scarf up to cover her ears and her mouth—partly to block the cold but mostly to block the smell of stale humanity drifting out of the alley.

Only money could bring her here. Money or the lack of it. But no more after tonight.

How many times had she made that same promise? Often enough for the words to become as hollow as her heart.

Neighbourhood kids ran past, growling at each other through plastic fangs and painted scowls. All innocence under evil facades. But not forever. Twenty years, tops, before face and mask traded places.

Cars passed steadily under flickering streetlights, tires bouncing in and out of slush-filled potholes. Good little husbands rushing home to good little wives. Enough to make Maggie want to puke.

An eighteen-wheeler sped too close to the curb, sending an icy rain in Maggie's direction. She jumped back with a yelp. Not fast enough. The dislodged slush painted her nylon-covered legs and dripped inside her knee-high boots. Like blood from a fresh wound. Only colder.

Hazard of the job. She knew that from the start. No reason to expect the end to be any different.

"You can't quit now." The ever-present voice jabbed at the side of Maggie's skull. "We're just getting started."

Maggie clenched her teeth. "Shut up. I'm not letting you take control this time."

The voice snickered. "Sweetheart, I'm always in control. You just have a problem with authority."

Maggie peered up and down the block, spotting no one. "Maybe so. But at least I've never killed anyone."

"Oh really? You should try it sometime. You'll find it

surprisingly liberating."

"Someone's coming."

"Bet you get to say that a lot."

Ignoring the voice, Maggie leaned her shoulders against the brick wall and tried to look dry. "Hi sugar," she said. "Want some company?"

The guy looked down his nose at her breasts. "How much?"

"Thirty-eight C," she said. "All natural. You interested or not?"

He rummaged through his coat pockets and pulled out a crumpled bill. "All I got is a fifty. What's that buy?"

"Cheapskate." The voice dug in Maggie's ear like an underfed flea.

She shook her head. "What's your name, fella?"

He looked around and shuffled on the spot. "Nothin'."

"That some kind of nickname?"

"Get it over with, Maggie. If you don't do it, I will."

"Joe," he said. "My name's Joe."

"Tell you what, Joe. Why don't you just take your fifty bucks, buy a nice present for your wife, and go home like a good little boy?"

"How you know I'm married?"

"You're all married."

"Let him give you the money, Maggie."

She jerked her head to the right and hissed. "Stay out of this."

Joe blinked. "Who you talking to?"

"Just go home, Joe. You don't want to be here."

"Oh crap. You're a cop. Oh man. Look, I never done this before. Won't do it again, either. I swear. Take the fifty. No, take it. Just don't tell anyone you saw me here."

She stared down at the crushed money in her hand, clenched it until the sweat of her palm softened its creases. "You shouldn't have done that."

The streetlights flared, bathing the night in an opalescent glow. Maggie faded into the pitch-dark alley. The voice emerged.

Joe's eyes flicked back and forth. A muted scream echoed behind his frozen lips.

"Hey, Joe. Time to find out what fifty bucks will get you."

THE RIGHT MAN
James S. Dorr

Mary, Mary. Mary Contrary—she had just been dumped, but life had to go on. She resented her old fiancé, naturally enough. In fact, she hated him for what he had done. Leading her on like that.

Taking advantage.

It was her curse, somehow, to end up with the wrong man every time, men like Arvin whom *she* should have dumped if she'd had more courage. If she had had more belief in herself.

Men like Arvin, she knew, had no future.

They had no careers, they just went from job to job. And, as she knew now—she'd known this before, too—from girlfriend to girlfriend.

She'd found them together. In bed together. "Arvin!" she'd screamed.

He had answered her, smooth as silk, "Mary, I told you never to let yourself in with your key like that, without knocking first."

Then he had dumped *her*.

"Mary," he had said, "we can't go on like this if you won't trust me."

But she had read somewhere: "Today is the first day of the rest of your life."

So it would be, she vowed.

Make lemonade from lemons, that was her motto—but more to the point, she got a new boyfriend.

His name was Giuseppe. He was everything Arvin was not. Tall, clean-shaven, smooth. He lived in a nicer part of the city—but not *too* nice. Not in so high-toned a neighbourhood that Mary felt out of place.

He wore suits and ties to work, not jeans like Arvin did. When Arvin *had* work.

But Mary realized, just like every cloud had a silver

lining, the reverse was true, too. Nothing was perfect.

"Giuseppe," she asked him once, "why are you out of town so many times? Sometimes on such short notice we have to break dates—dates I've looked forward to."

"Mary, Mary," he said. He kissed her. "Mary, you know I'm disappointed, too. But it's the business. You know how it is, you start at the bottom, you work your way up. Right now, it's me that has to go out of town, go on the business trips. That's what the boss says. But one of these days, you'll see, I'll work myself up. I'll be a boss myself, then other guys'll have to go out of town."

Mary kissed him back. Giuseppe had such a romantic accent—the way he talked was like a movie she'd once seen on TV. Something on the *Lifetime* channel, movies they made just for women like her.

That was the first time she let Giuseppe get his hands in her bra. Giuseppe was like that, always a gentleman. Never trying to move too fast for her, never doing anything like that with her until he was sure he had her okay first.

Not like Arvin.

Giuseppe told her once, "It comes from being a Catholic. I mean from being raised as a Catholic, to have respect for women like you. For *ladies* like you."

That was the time she gave him her okay to do a lot more than just get his hands on her titties.

She had a job, too, a dime store sales job. Well, not a dime store literally anymore, but she worked behind a counter. Cosmetics and perfumes.

She got samples sometimes, new products the drummers would bring around to sell. She and the other salesgirls would try them on, then she'd go back to the apartment Giuseppe and she now shared when he was in town. It was a bigger place than she could afford alone, but she insisted on chipping in something, even though Giuseppe had told her he'd rather go the whole rent by himself. He was sweet that way.

By now the two of them practically were engaged, but

not quite engaged yet. Giuseppe was sweet about things that way, too. He admitted he wasn't sure he was ready to make that big a commitment yet or that, he suspected, she was either. Even though she *was*. He said he didn't want to hurt her, if things didn't work out.

Not like Arvin, she thought, still seething. Still remembering—her humiliation when he had dumped *her*. This was after *he* had insisted they be engaged—even though he'd never bought her a ring—using it as an excuse to get them shacking up together, even though she had wanted to wait. She'd wanted to get to know him better.

And not like Arvin had been the first, either.

But with Giuseppe, well, she knew he was a man of honour. She didn't know everything about him yet, but that was part of the fun of romance. She had met his mother—his father was deceased, some kind of accident that the family didn't like to talk about, which she could understand. As for the mother, she was sort of shifty-eyed—some sort of tic that made it hard for her to look directly at Mary—but she was open and warm and friendly. Very "Old World," with an accent like her son's, but a lot stronger. Very religious, with crosses on the walls.

But to the point, at Mary's work they sometimes got cosmetic samples, which she'd try on and show to Giuseppe. He had taste that way. He could tell her which lines would sell, which ones made her look ladylike, as opposed to those what weren't so good, that perhaps were too garish—that just made her look cheap. She used what he told her in her job sometimes, steering customers to products that would be the best selections for them. Telling them also what to avoid, but telling them why, too, and always showing them what would be better. Leaving them happy and ready, the next time, to come back to her counter for their next purchases.

Her boss noticed this and gave her a raise—over and above her commissions. He also gave her a promotion, along with the afternoon off to celebrate.

Mary went home to share the good news, but Giuseppe wasn't there. Of course, she thought. He'd still be at work.

Then it occurred to her she didn't really know where it was he worked, where his office was those times he wasn't being sent out of town.

She rarely went through his drawers or his closet—in fact, she never did. Unlike some that she'd had in the past, this was a relationship that *was* based on trust, and when Giuseppe had asked her when she moved in to leave his personal things alone—"It's just man stuff, you know," he had said, "things that wouldn't interest a lady like you"—she'd been okay with that. But now she wondered . . . perhaps there was an address somewhere or a phone number she could use to call him.

But then their own phone rang.

She had, of course, wondered at times if there might be some other woman that he was seeing, those times he was out of town. But he wasn't out of town all that often, and it was becoming less and less often now, as he had told her once or twice of advancements in *his* work, just like he had promised.

"I'll work myself up," he'd said, "then other guys'll have to go out of town."

Still her hand trembled, just a little, as she picked up the phone.

What if the call was from a woman?

But it was no woman. The voice belonged to a man who called himself Angelo. "What is this?" Angelo said. "Has Giuseppe got some kind of answering service or something?"

"Uh—uh, sort of," Mary said. "This is Mary. If you'd like, I can take a message."

"Yeah? Well, okay, Mary. Normally I wouldn't just talk to anyone like this, but Giuseppe's mentioned a 'Mary' to me once, and anyway this is sort of an emergency. Like they could get someone local to do it, but usually we like it to be someone from out of town, like it's harder to trace it that way, you know?"

Mary didn't know quite what to say. "Uh—uh, yeah," she stammered.

"Well, good. So you tell Giuseppe this, that Angelo called and he should call back if there's any problems. He knows the number. I need him to get on a plane to Detroit—the first one he can get out of La Guardia. I got a job for him."

Mary wrote this down. "Uh, sure."

"Good. You tell him that Angelo owes him a favour then—a *big* favour. If there's anything one of the guys from Detroit can do for him . . ."

Mary wrote that down, too. "Sure, Angelo. I'll see that he knows."

She wasn't stupid. She had watched movies on TV other than just romances on the *Lifetime* channel those nights when Giuseppe was out of town. She went to their bedroom and to his closet, the one he had for himself, and got a chair to stand on when she looked on the shelf. She got a flashlight so she could see better as she moved some old coats or something out of the way to see what was behind them.

She knew better than to touch anything, so she just gaped when her light caught the glint of blue gunmetal.

She forced the issue. She gave the message to Giuseppe when he came in a half hour later, and knew that he knew she wasn't stupid. While he was in Detroit, she went to the library and looked up newspapers and books as well. She wasn't surprised when he got back home the evening after and greeted her with an armload of roses.

"Mary, put on your nice clothes. I'd like us to go out to eat tonight, anywhere you suggest."

She nodded. "There's a new place that's just opened up I've been thinking about. We might go there."

She paused and gulped. "Giuseppe, we've got to talk."

"I know," he said. "But not till we get there."

She nodded again. Then, over dinner, she told him about her past. About Arvin. About before Arvin. About her bad luck in romance before *then*. "Giuseppe," she said, "I've thought, with you, that lightning had finally struck. You know what I mean? Like in you I've found the right man for me, finally. But now, with this . . ."

Giuseppe winced. "Mary," he started, "it's not what you think—"

Mary shook her head. "It *is* what I think. But that's not the point. Giuseppe, it's time that we stopped having secrets from each other, that we finally made a commitment—that's what *I* think. That we should start talking about getting married."

"You mean you want us to be engaged? In spite of. . ."

She nodded. "Yes."

Giuseppe leaned over the table and kissed her, then broke into a grin. "Mary, I've *wanted* to ask you. You don't know how much—except I was afraid. You know, my profession . . ."

"All I know is you're getting advancements, isn't that right? Just like you promised. That pretty soon you'll be a sub-boss or something and won't have to go out on the road so much?"

He nodded himself now. "But—do you mind that I don't have a ring to give you? That is, not on me. I mean, tomorrow we can pick one out. Maybe a ring for every finger if that's what you'd like. But do you mind, Mary, if I ask you to marry me right now?"

Mary had trouble holding back tears, she was so happy. "Of course I don't mind." She took a deep breath. "And as for a ring, I don't need a ring.

"But there is something else . . ."

"Yes?" Giuseppe said.

"Well," she said, "it's about your friend Angelo. You know, from Detroit—that owes you a favour?" She rummaged in her purse. "I've still got a picture of Arvin here somewhere, and I was thinking. For his first contract . . ."

IN THE THIRD PERSON

Everett C. Gavel, Jr.

I rip you open
and tear you apart,
I taste those little pieces
As I devour your heart,
Your love for me,
This love forbidden,
Your feelings for me,
They should have stayed hidden,
Never break those chains,
Do not come near,
Or what you have now,
Will not remain dear.

STRANGER IN THE NIGHT

Krys Douglas

Jake and Chet stumbled out of their senior prom at 4:20 a.m.; their dates, disgusted, had dumped them at two o'clock. They stood on the sidewalk in front of the Mason Hotel.

"Man, you got us bounced," Jake said as he shoved his friend to make a point about how drunk Chet was.

Struggling to keep his balance, Chet flailed out, grabbing the first thing his hand touched—Mrs. Garotzi's fur-clad arm. She, too, was leaving the hotel. "Sorry, ma'am." Chet slurred.

"Sorry," Jake echoed.

Mrs. Garotzi looked them over carefully. They stared blearily back at her. She was perhaps forty, and tall. Dark hair held back by jewelled clips framed her olive complexion. The mink coat fell back to reveal a black dress set off by a single ruby pendant. Had either young man known anything about fashion, he would have recognized the simplicity of Versace; instead they gawked at the voluptuous figure it encased.

"You boys should not be out so late in this condition," she said, her English tinged with an accent.

"Jus' left the prom, ma'am," Jake said.

"Kicked out," Chet added. "Said we wuz drunk."

"Yes," Mrs. Garotzi said. "Well, it's not safe downtown when you're like this; let me take you back to my house. I'll sober you up then send you home in my car." She gestured to the sleek Rolls Royce that glided up to the curb.

Chet and Jake looked at each other, grins spreading across their faces. "Mrs. Robinson." Jake silently mouthed the words as both climbed into the car.

The ride was largely silent. Both boys, after initial attempts at small talk, were tongue-tied by the woman who lounged against the seat and gazed at them provocatively through half-closed eyes.

Now they stood in the living room of her home. Candles on the mantelpiece provided the light; heavy drapes covered the windows. The dark furniture seemed to close in upon them. Chet and Jake nervously looked at their hostess. Her dark eyes glittered, her red lips parted to reveal white teeth.

"Sit, please," she said.

"Er, I think . . ." Chet began.

"We really should go home," Jake said.

Mrs. Garotzi swirled a dark red liquid in a glass and walked toward them. "Come, now, just stay for a short time." Her voice was low and seductive.

Jake automatically stepped backward and tripped on a footstool; as he fell, he grasped the curtain. It pulled away from the window, and the first rays of the rising sun penetrated the room. Mrs. Garotzi put up an arm to shield her face from the light and screamed. As the shaft of sunlight struck, her body withered, became skeletal.

"Oh, God," Chet said. "Oh, God."

"Jeeze," Jake said. "She sure looks older in the sunlight."

PORTRAIT OF A HUSBAND
Gail Kavanagh

It was said that Madolyn and Anthony were the perfect couple, although it was Madolyn who said it most often.

She never tired of describing their first meeting. They had been students, she studying art, he economics. He had pursued her with champagne, roses, and midnight strolls along the riverbank. She had kept the wretched man waiting for weeks while she dithered about his proposal. She wanted to be an artist. Should she fulfill her ambition or her womanhood?

She chose marriage, and Anthony was the happiest man in the world. So Madolyn said.

For, in spite of being the happiest man and the most lavishly adored husband in the world, Anthony was a dour man. He had charming eyes as soft and brown as a Spaniel pup and a trace of sensuality about the contours of his mouth, but for the most part people in their circle regarded him as a dull stick.

If he had once been the passionate lover Madolyn described, their friends could see no sign of it now. After fifteen years of marriage, not a whiff of scandal had disturbed Madolyn's domestic pond. Anthony was always to be seen standing doggedly at her side through the seasonal round of parties and picking up the tab on her shopping trips.

They were not extravagantly rich, but he had made some prudent investments when young. They sent their children to good schools, owned a charming house, and could afford to support a woman with Madolyn's good taste. She bought only the very best, on the assertion that it was timeless, never went out of style, and was therefore good value for money. Many privately thought she had chosen Anthony for the same reasons.

So for fifteen years, the pond remained undisturbed.

Then fate cast its first stone.

It began at a reception for Gabriella di Franco, the Italian-born artist, whose vibrant canvasses had shaken the art world like a cyclone. Her own beauty was almost as startling. She was a tall, red-haired Amazon with green eyes and a stunning figure. Anthony was clearly mesmerized. Madolyn caught him staring at the artist as if she were one of her own paintings and he were calculating whether he would have enough left over from the budget to buy her.

Soon the two were deep in conversation. Gabriella di Franco had a way of oozing over a man like honey over a warm muffin. Anthony's eyes looked more Spaniel-like than ever, and his mouth shaped itself into distinctly sensual lines.

"Darling," Madolyn murmured, "why don't you introduce me to Miss di Franco?"

Gabriella regarded her with scant interest.

"Your husband is very attractive," she said in a voice redolent of late nights and men's eyes. "I would like very much to paint him."

"You don't do portraits," Madolyn snapped.

"Every artist does portraits," Gabriella said with an artful toss of her flaming hair.

After the reception, Madolyn and Gabriella never had cause to meet socially again. But worrying little snippets of gossip would catch up with Madolyn. Anthony had been seen going into the building where Gabriella was renting a large studio apartment; Gabriella was delaying her return to Rome for unknown reasons; someone saw her walking with Anthony along the riverbank. He did not smell of Gabriella's perfume or come home late with lame excuses, and Madolyn never found an auburn hair on his clothing no matter how hard she looked, yet there was something about him that disturbed her. Only another wife, she reflected bitterly, would understand, but she wasn't going to give those harpies any more fuel for their gossip.

A week before their sixteenth anniversary, Madolyn called Anthony at his office. To her annoyance, his assistant Miss Bloomfield was off sick and a temp took the call.

"I'm afraid Mr. Harvey is out," the temp said. "Can I take a message?"

"Just tell him that his wife called and will call again later," Madolyn replied. "It isn't urgent."

"Certainly, Mrs. Harvey. Oh, by the way, did you get the flowers?"

"Flowers?" Madolyn said blankly. "What flowers?"

"One dozen red roses—I'm afraid I got the inscription on the card wrong. Mr. Harvey asked me to put 'To Gabriella, to mark our first meeting,' and I asked them to put 'for our anniversary.' But of course that might not be the same thing at all. I am so sorry."

"No, that's perfectly all right," Madolyn said and quickly hung up.

She stared at the phone for a while then, with slow and deliberate movements, she went upstairs and dressed carefully to go out.

She caught a taxi to Gabriella's apartment, not wishing anyone to see her car parked nearby. Gabriella herself answered the door, wearing a paint-spattered denim shirt, a pair of baggy pants rolled up to the knees, and her hair pulled back into a ponytail. She looked sensational.

"Why, Mrs. Harvey," she purred. "How nice."

"This isn't a social visit," Madolyn said, wishing her voice would remain steady. "I want to speak to you about my husband."

Gabriella stood aside and motioned Madolyn to enter. She followed the artist up a flight of stairs to a huge, sunlit studio. Several half-completed canvasses in the familiar vibrant style were ranged around the walls. In the centre of the room was an easel, covered in a white sheet.

"I am very busy, as you can see," Gabriella said. "But I can spare you a few moments."

"Thank you." Madolyn felt horribly ill at ease, but she couldn't turn back now. Something in her very bones told her that Anthony had been here.

"There's been gossip," she said. "I have been told that Anthony has been seen entering your apartment, not once, but many times."

"Ah . . ." Gabriella nodded wisely. "Gossip, such a bore. I prefer to avoid people when I can. So many of them have nothing better to do than talk about others. You imagine that your husband and I are having an affair?"

"Are you?"

"My dear, would you believe me if I said no? If course not," Gabriella went on, not waiting for an answer. "Your husband is a very attractive man, so naturally you fear that another woman will steal him from you. I quite understand. I am a woman, too, as well as an artist."

"And I was an artist, long ago." Madolyn glanced around the studio and inhaled the smell of oils and turpentine with a pang.

"I could never give it up for a mere man," Gabriella said. "But I see you are troubled, and it seems I must tell you the truth, even though Anthony has begged me not to reveal his reason for coming here."

Madolyn gasped aloud. "So it is true!"

"But of course. He comes here every day."

"But why, what are you doing together?"

"Is it not obvious? I am painting his portrait. A special portrait. It is intended as an anniversary gift for you."

As light dawned, Madolyn gave a gasp of delight and considerable relief.

"A portrait! How charming." She looked at the easel. "Is that it? Can I look?"

"Certainly not," Gabriella said. "You mustn't see it yet."' A sharp ringing interrupted her, and she clucked her tongue. "Now the phone—do people think I have nothing to do all day? I won't be a moment." She hurried out of the studio, and Madolyn could hear her speaking into the phone.

She glanced longingly at the easel. Surely a quick peek wouldn't hurt. Carefully, she lifted a corner of the white sheet and raised it enough to see the portrait. She stared, her eyes bulging, and quickly dropped it again.

"I am sorry," Gabriella said, sweeping back into the studio. "I have to go down to the gallery at once. I trust your curiosity has been satisfied?"

Madolyn thought for a moment that Gabriella knew she had been peeking, but it seemed she was only referring to the reason for her visit.

"Yes, thank you," she said. "Quite satisfied. I can't wait to see the portrait."

"I'm sure you can't," Gabriella said cryptically and ushered her down the stairs.

Once outside, Madolyn headed for the nearest café and found a secluded table. She fanned her flaming cheeks with the menu and reflected on what she had seen under the sheet in Gabriella's studio. How could he? Naked! Lying on a red couch without a stitch on, a bunch of grapes in one hand and a glass of champagne in the other. Shameless! And that hussy, posing him like that.

Fanning herself even harder, Madolyn ordered coffee then stared unseeingly at the café walls. *My God,* she thought, *is that how Anthony looks to that woman?*

Stripped of his sombre suits and hangdog look, freed from his twenty-four-hour obsession with expense accounts and tax havens, yes, he did look like that. Really, when she thought about it, it was a most romantic gesture, to give a wife of fifteen years a nude portrait of oneself. She could just see it hanging over their bed. Certainly none of her friends would ever have received such a gift. She could imagine how she would tease them with hints about it. Perhaps she would even allow one or two of them to see it, if they could be trusted to keep their hands off Anthony afterwards.

The days passed. She ignored the gossip. Gabriella finally departed for Rome, and Madolyn's pond settled into tranquility again.

On the day of their anniversary, the Harveys held a small dinner party for their closest friends. It was a great success, and all the guests commented on the good looks of their host and hostess.

At the end of the meal, Anthony rose and called for attention.

"Darling," he addressed Madolyn. "It's time to present my gift to you. I have been keeping it in my study all day, so if you will excuse me, I'll just slip out and fetch it. Gordon, would you give me a hand, old chap? It's rather large."

Madolyn watched him leave the room with his burly friend in tow, and her cheeks burned. Surely he wasn't going to give her the portrait in front of all their friends? Had he no shame? In exquisite discomfort, she watched as he and Gordon came back into the room, carrying the portrait still shrouded in its white sheet. They lifted it up onto the buffet and rested it against the wall.

"I hope you like it, darling," Anthony said. "If nothing else, it will be a good investment for the future. An original di Franco is sure to increase in value." With a flourish, he pulled away the sheet.

The guests clapped their hands and exclaimed their surprise and delight. Madolyn grasped the edge of the table, straining her mouth into a smile, her face betraying nothing.

It was a magnificent portrait, painted in deeper colours than Gabriella normally used. Anthony had the look of a brooding, Goyaesque figure. But it wasn't the painting she had seen in the studio.

This Anthony was fully clothed.

TANGO OF TEARS

Gretchen Wilsenach

With lonely abandon, she accepts the invitation
Sadness hidden, provocation seductive
Hands holding his, careless nonchalance
Knees mutate to cello, bowing his legs
Rhythm impels their meld, a jukebox rhapsody
His eyes, darkly fired daggers, frenzied begging
Her straps slip soft, white flesh
Backless dress clinging, like welded lips
Slit high, one thigh exposed, silken ebon's sheath
He senses shocking azure mirrors
She seeks a pleasing countenance
Deep within, heart yearns for solace
The night his—paid for.
The loving hers—died for.

KEEPSAKE
Diana Woods

I pull on my red dress, sequins dipping into my cleavage and fringe licking my thighs. In rhinestone-studded stilettos, I pirouette in front of a mirror. No man can resist me, I tell myself, as pheromones blanket the air. At age thirty-nine with platinum hair, I like 'em young and wild.

When I saunter into the marina club, the band's playing. I grab the last seat at the bar, squeezing between two men. "I'm Sheila. How are ya?"

I end up with two drinks and arms doubled over the back of my chair. "I'm Bill," the younger one with the red hair and freckles says. He shoves his pinkie into my armpit and laughs.

"Call me Dale," the other says. His left hand is missing half a ring finger. I'm thinking jealous lover, but he talks about a work injury, rambles on about manufacturing and dangerous machinery as if I care.

Several beers later, we're friends, but I don't plan to take either of them home. They'll hope until the bar closes. I keep my options open.

"Anyone dance?" I ask, looking sideways. These hardcore drinkers, they rarely do. Makes it easy for me to meet other guys. I tie a sweater on the back of my chair. Dale keeps his arm over my empty seat.

Men ask me to dance as I sit at the bar with Bill and Dale. If I were off standing alone, looking hungry, they'd avoid me. It's a guy ego thing, nothing to do with me. But, tonight, I'll do the picking.

"Watch my drink, Billy." Or maybe Dale? "I'll be back in a minute." If it's an hour later, they won't notice. They're busy doing the guy bonding thing, talking about babes like me.

As I edge over to the dance floor to check out the crowd, a pack of men clear a path. Most of these guys date men in the band. I like their soft hair and polished fingernails, but tonight I'm prowling for tall, dark and manly.

When my fingers slide across the back of a white silk shirt, I have a premonition that he's it. His body feels sturdy, full of energy. I like the bulk of his arms, the breadth of his shoulders, the way the muscles in his neck braid as he turns his head to face me. I grab his hand and yank him onto the dance floor.

"What's your name?" I ask.

"Reno," he says with a grin.

As we dance, crushed sequins fall on our feet like confetti. We're tight with the torsos. When the music quickens, he spins me under his arm. I pivot on one heel and end up staring at his butt. The man can dance. I'll give him that.

"I'll buy you a drink," he says at the end of the set.

As we approach the bar, I wave to Billy and Dale. They're hoping I'll be hot and ready for them soon. I can see it in their eyes and their empty glasses.

"What'll you have?" Reno asks.

"Tequila sunrise." I can drink plenty of those. Reno nibbles my bait, but it'll be hours before we stumble out to the street. With my roving eyes, I might leave with another guy.

"Live around the marina?" Reno asks. I imagine that he thinks about following me home.

"Yeah, close by. What about you?" Not that I care. I wasn't going in his direction.

"Ocean Park," he says. Closer than I'd like, but he wouldn't be in my neighbourhood for long. It won't be love full of keepsake memories, just long hard thrusts and a crumpled bed.

I'm itching to have him, but it's too early to leave. I follow a routine, a long warm-up then the finale. I watch his liquor. His performance is critical.

We dance for a couple hours, feet stomping, hips grinding. His laser-like eyes invade every part of my body.

The flesh sizzles where his beam lingers. Heat rises inside me. He pulls me close and licks my earlobes as his fingers hike the mounds on my chest. I'm ready to go. He's had enough to drink.

The arrangements are easy. He didn't drive. After my invitation, he waves off his friends and follows me into the parking garage. Under the glare of the outdoor lighting, he looks even younger, but he doesn't act like a kid the way Bill did.

As he slides onto the seat of my Mustang, he asks, "How old are you?"

"Does it matter?" I answer. He laughs and stretches his arm around my shoulder. I put my hand on his leg. Stops the questions for a moment.

As I turn onto my street, he glances at the sign. When I pull into the driveway, he seems anxious. I worry that he'll balk. My time wasted on him.

"Do you live alone?" he asks.

"My son's at his dad's house tonight."

I know what he's thinking. He wants the sex, but paranoia kicks in. I walk him through the living room, the kitchen and into my room. When he sees the empty bed, his face turns red and eager.

He yanks off his shirt, buttons and all. A jerk of his wrist and his khakis slide down his legs. He wears boxer shorts, not the spandex briefs that overheat testicles. I grab the elastic band and tug his shorts to the floor. Then he peels off my red dress and backs me onto the bed.

The rest is all the same. His hot breath on my neck. His warm, sweaty skin. His fingers walking my belly. "I want you, baby," he moans. That's what they all do. It's what I expect, but with this man, something different happens deep inside me.

After he rolls over, I recline on my back, legs bent and knees pressed together.

"Hey baby! Why so stiff?" he asks.

I look straight into his eyes. "Thanks for the payload, honey."

"What do you mean?" Then he gets it.

I see the tadpoles swimming in his eyes. He'd like to recapture all of them, but thousands are foraging up my channel. Will he curse or bring on his fists? I arch my abdomen to rush the migrating herd.

His eyes lock on to my belly. He can't help his instincts. Men are like that. Nakedness changes the way their brain thinks.

"What the hell," he says as he jumps back on top. An extra batch can't hurt, I tell myself.

After the door slams, I pluck his boxer shorts from under the bed. They'll be part of the story that I tell my child.

"And that's how I met your dad, honey. He left you a keepsake."

OVERSHADOWED
Betty Dobson

The inside was dark. Immutable blackness filled the kitchen but couldn't overshadow Estella's memories.

She brushed away a stray tear, oblivious to the streak of dirt left on her cheek. Nothing had gone as planned. She'd been so wrong about everything.

Brian was just as dead.

Moonlight cast a spectral glow that crept through the windows as the clouds slipped away. The night turned bright and hollow. The wind outside the broken window sounded like claws on gravel.

Making a split second decision, she retrieved the boning knife and ran for the front door.

The car keys jangled in her coat pocket. If she moved fast enough, she just might get away.

At the doorway, she looked up. Fresh clouds drifted across the full moon's leering face, casting the night back into darkness.

Time to run.

But her eyes hadn't adjusted yet. She couldn't see the car. Couldn't see anything. She blinked a few times—nothing but black.

Slowly, the night bled pools of grey, revealing the rounded silhouette of her Lexus, broken only by the stabbing outline of the open trunk. So close. She closed her eyes and inhaled deeply. A quick sprint would get her there. Nothing to it.

A skritch on tile. A breeze of movement past her ear. And the lights went out again, like a blind drawn over her eyes.

"Going somewhere?" The voice hissed in her ear, low but familiar. "We're just getting started."

Her heart dipped low in her chest. She'd been wrong

about Brian—wrong about everything—but the damage was already done.

"Come on, Estella." Booze-soaked breath stung her cheek. "You know what I want. You know what to say."

"Bite me."

"First things first." A swampy tongue trailed along her jaw line. "Say it. Should be easy. I know you read all those notes I sent."

"Okay." Estella eased back into the strange embrace. Red and yellow strobes flashed under her lids. A fresh migraine sliced through her left eye. "I love you."

A hard sigh buffeted her neck. "That's better. Don't you feel better?"

Estella slid her forearms up along the intruder's legs. "Not quite."

"More?" The blinding hand dropped away from her eyes. "Aren't you a treasure?"

"Just practical. There's no need for this to get ugly."

"That's one opinion."

Estella forced herself to take long, slow breaths. In through the nose. Out through the mouth. Four more. Three more.

Gloved hand raised slightly on two.

And down hard on one.

Her attacker screamed as the boning knife tore through flesh and struck bone.

Free of his unwelcome embrace, Estella turned toward him, twisting the blade as she moved, shifting it deeper into soft tissue. "That's for making me doubt Brian, you pervert. He'd still be alive if it weren't for you."

"So modest," he said. His words oozed out between clenched teeth. "You know it wasn't me. Never even met the guy."

"Well, you're about to." She yanked out the knife and drove it into the man's chest.

His eyes popped open as he reached instinctively for her wrist—and his limp fingers barely brushed her arm on the way down.

Estella smiled even as fresh tears blotted out the sight of his body. *Guess it's true,* she thought, relief slowly overtaking her grief over Brian. *Killing's easier the second time around. At least this one deserved to die.*

HOT DESIRE (CONCRETE POEM)
Brenda Roberts

L u s t f l a m e s u p
l i k e T e x a s
— t h e d r y
hot
desire
consumes me.

Writhing on
glass-shard sands,
eyes closed to
clouds rising overhead,
hot and cold
slam together
creating a funnel
inhaling
all
thoughts like
debris tossed airborne.

Touching

grasping

clinging

riding wave

after ShoCkwave of
orgasmic delight

dropping to reality
in a roller coaster of
please!

more!
nomore don't s t o p

Tornadic
devastating
passionate
desire
releases
minds one
single
touch;
petal soft
roses
left of
cacti prickles —

pain from pleasure
throbs into focus:

I
want
you.

TO HOLD 'EM OR FOLD 'EM
Gary R. Hoffman

If music has charms to soothe the savage beast, I was really wishing for two things right now. One was a mitt full of quarters. The other was a jukebox I listened to all the time at Smitty's Bar and Grill. The guy who was standing in front of me and shaking from nervousness was holding what appeared to be a very large gun—like maybe a small cannon. In reality, it was probably a .38, but the barrel looks a lot bigger when it's pointed straight at you.

"Now, Mr. Higgins, let's be calm and talk about this."

"Ain't nothin' to talk about. You're here to take me back to jail, and I'm not goin'."

"Mr. Higgins, I'm not a bounty hunter. I'm a private detective. If you'll let me get my wallet out of my fanny pack, I'll prove it to you."

"Your what?"

Oh, crap! Why didn't I just carry a purse like most other women? "My fanny pack. This thing hanging on my side." I tried to motion towards it with my head while holding my hands in the air. I figured if I put my hands down, it might be the last act of my life, and I had other fantasies about what that act was going to be. It would probably involve Tony Marsalis, and I would be screaming his name.

"If you're not a bounty hunter, what are you doin' here?"

"Like I said, I'm a private detective. Your mother hired me to find you."

"My mother?"

"Yes, your mother. She wants to talk to you."

He let the gun fall to his side. I slowly lowered my hands.

"What about?"

"I have no idea. She just hired me to find you and

deliver the message."

He shook his head and scratched his chin with his non-gun hand. "Probably wants me to give myself up. I told her before I ain't goin' back to jail. I done nothin' wrong, this time."

"Well, I delivered the message. Can I go now?"

He was looking at the floor, and he waved me out with his gun hand. I backed up slowly to the door, turned, and ran like a scared rabbit, which was a pretty good description of me at the time. I had a hard time turning the key in the ignition because I was shaking so much. The sweat on my hands didn't help either. Ray Higgins' mother didn't quite paint a picture of him as a fugitive. It was more like they had a family spat, and she couldn't locate him, so she hired me. Maybe my dad was right. He always said I was out of my element—and mind.

My dad had been a beat cop for over twenty years in St. Louis. He was savvier about the world than I was. My mom passed away a few years ago. Having spent some time in front of a gun, again, I vowed to go see him more. I then wondered how many times I had made that vow. I have lots of brothers and sisters who go to see him on a regular basis, so I could easily rationalize my way out of that argument.

My name's Meg Bartlett. I've been a private dick going on eight years now. Worked all of that time in St. Louis. I grew up there and had lots of contacts there, so it seemed logical for me to stay, but days like this, nothing seemed logical. Smitty's Bar was just a few blocks from my apartment, so I headed there. I needed something very alcoholic to get my body back to semi-normal. Smitty's old jukebox was cranking out Jimmy singing "Margaritaville." Sounded like an omen to me, and breaking omens can be bad luck. I wasn't really sure if that was true or not, but why take a chance? I ordered a margarita.

I only got down two or three sips when someone tapped me on the shoulder. I was half hoping for it to be

Tony Marsalis, and the good half of me was hoping it was someone else. I had this thing about Tony. I thought he used me in the sack, but I guess I used him about as much as he used me. He was just someone I had a hard time staying away from. I spun around on the bar stool and stared into the face of someone I absolutely did not know.

"You Meg Bartlett?" he asked.

"And who are you, sir?"

He stuck his hand out for me to shake. "Name's Jake Cash. No relation to Johnny, before you ask. I was told I might find you here. I've been trying to call you, but a recording keeps telling me the number is no longer in service."

Okay, now it dawned on me what else I was supposed to pay out in bills last month. I knew I had missed something but couldn't figure out what. Maybe it was one of those things that I just really didn't want to pay. Thinking back on it, that may be why I had that extra money for those great shoes I found at The Galleria. Oh, well. "Yes, I'm Meg Bartlett. How can I help you?"

"I need to talk to you."

I looked at the back booth on the left. It was empty. "Yeah, let's take that booth in the back." I used that booth to talk to most of my clients anyway. My office wasn't quite as presentable as Smitty's Bar. And I had no real way to listen to all the great music on Smitty's jukebox. "So, Mr. Cash, what can I do for you?"

"First, call me Jake." He laid a picture that looked like a mug shot with the numbers cut off on the table. "Second, help me find this guy."

Oh, oh! Red flag time! Didn't I just about soil my panties over a situation like this? "And who is this guy?" I didn't pick up the picture, like that somehow would protect me.

"He's my brother-in-law."

"And you can't find him because . . . ?"

"He just didn't come home from work three nights ago.

My sister's going crazy. I told her I'd try and help find him. I looked around a few places where he used to hang out, but no luck. I really need to get back to work myself. A friend of mine told me about you, so I thought I'd let you handle it."

Ah, word of mouth advertising! The best! And the cheapest. "Okay, Jake. I'll need two thousand for the first week. More if expenses get out of hand."

To my surprise, he pulled out a roll of hundred dollar bills. Twenty of them hit the table. I gratefully gathered them up and got the rest of the information from Jake. He left, and I took my margarita back to the bar to finish it. Before I left, I flashed the picture at Walley, one of the bartenders at Smitty's. "Seen this guy in here?"

"Not again," he said and shook his head no. I always felt it was good to start with the first person I had a chance to question. Walley had never given me any good answers, but I always tried, just in case. I downed the last of my afternoon pick-me-up and headed out the door to find a guy named Norman Eugene Bolinski. I really didn't have much to go on. Jake said his sister had gone to stay with a friend of hers in Kansas City, so I could probably only talk to her on the phone. I thought that was kind of strange, but different people handle difficult situations in different ways. I figured my best way to start might be with the police. I had made friends with a detective named Mel Kirkland on one of my other cases, so I went to visit him first.

He ran the name through the system. To my surprise, he found four people with that name in the United States. Two were dead. One lived in New York, and one lived in Denver. He did find the name used as an alias by a guy named Norman Eugene Boyle. Boyle was arrested in Kansas City on a charge of passing fraudulent checks. Apparently, he stayed around Kansas City for a few weeks, according to his parole officer, but then he quit reporting to his PO and disappeared from the police radar. The only thing that clicked with me was the fact that he started in KC and his wife was there now. So I now went to find my next best source of information.

On my way to find him, I stopped at a Walgreen's and used their fantastic little machine to make several copies of the picture I had of Norm Bolinski. I knew my contact would want some.

Condie was a person who always seemed to be on the streets of St. Louis, somewhere. I had no idea what his real name was. I only knew he got his nickname from putting condiments on everything he ate, and at least half the time when I talked to him, he was eating. No one seemed to know or care where he got the money to keep eating.

I located him down on Washington Avenue, sitting in the outdoor part of one of the new restaurants there called Quinton's. He had a pile of onion rings in front of him covered with cheese and what looked like some kind of chilli or salsa. He was cranking the hell out of a pepper mill when I walked up to his table and laid down a picture with a twenty dollar bill sticking out from underneath it.

He looked up and smiled when he saw me. "Megan, my dear." He looked down at the picture. "Don't know the dude, but I do know something about the guy underneath him." He pulled out the twenty and put it in his shirt pocket. "Now, have a seat and tell me how I may be of service to you."

"Need to find this guy."

"Now that part I already figured out. What you know about him?"

"May use the name Norm Boyle or Norm Bolinski. Supposedly disappeared three days ago." I got more pictures from my fanny pack, plus a couple of hundred in twenties, and laid them on the table. I had done this enough to know the drill. Condie wanted bribe money for people who might know something about this person.

Condie picked up an onion ring and carefully inserted it into his mouth. He chewed for a few seconds. "So how have you been, darlin'?"

"Fine. Looks like you're still doing okay."

"Oh, I get by. I get by." Another dripping onion ring went into his mouth.

I knew nothing else was going to get done right then. I checked my watch, and it was quitting time for me today. Actually, one of the perks of my job is setting my own hours, at least most of the time, so today my hours ended now.

The next morning, I dressed very casually—jeans, loose t-shirt, a funky uplift bra, and tennis shoes—like most other days and took off to see where this Norm Bolinski and his wife lived. I finally ran down their building superintendent, who was fixing a sink in one of the units. "Yeah, they moved in about a week ago. Signed a year's lease on one of our furnished units. Paid first and last months' rent. Not sure I ever saw Mrs. Bolinski. He was in and out a lot though."

"Mind if I talk to some of their neighbours?"

"Knock yourself out. Probably the only one home right now would be Mrs. Valendez in 3B. Everybody else should be at work."

I got a "Just a minute!" when I knocked on the door of 3B. Several seconds later, a stooped-over, grey haired lady using a walker opened the door, wide. This told me it must be a pretty safe building.

I introduced myself; she invited me in; offered to fix me tea, which I declined; and proceeded to tell me she really didn't know anything about the Bolinskis except that she never saw a woman there. I showed her the picture I had of Mr. Bolinski. "You know, I don't think that's the man I saw over there. The man I saw was older. Had a more receding hairline." Jake Cash had a very receding hairline! I thanked her for her time and left.

As I was leaving the building, I wanted to make a left, but there was a line of traffic in that lane. So I turned right. I wasn't too good to go around the block to avoid waiting. Of course, I checked my rear view mirror immediately, because in the city you never know what kind of nut might be driving ninety behind you. I only saw one car pull out from the curb behind me. I pushed a CD into my player. Willie started telling me I was on the road again. I just wished he were telling me which road I should take. Norman Eugene Bolinski might be running around St. Louis, but I didn't have a clue where. Mel was going to call me if anything came through the police department about him. I knew Condie would call if he found out anything. I checked my watch, and it was too early for Tony to call or even show up at Smitty's, so I did something I really didn't want to do. I took some of the money Jake gave me and paid my telephone bill, plus a penalty to get it reinstalled. I could never figure out how it cost the phone company seventy-five dollars to flip a little switch again. At least they didn't charge me to turn the switch off.

I then decided to do something I seldom do. It's not that it's illegal or immoral or anything, it's just that I really don't like to do it. I went back to my apartment to clean and dust! I was just starting to get out what few cleaning supplies I had when my cell phone rang. Even if it was a wrong number, they were going to get a lot of attention.

I heard Condie's voice. "Quinton's. PDQ." The line went dead. If Condie had been in front of me, I would have kissed his cheese-covered lips! I was saved from housework!

Condie was outside again. He had a sandwich in front of him that was indistinguishable as to its origin. All kinds of sauces were streaming over the sides, concealing any kind of meat that may have been in there. "Word on the street is that your boy is staying at a rooming house. 224 Salisbury." He slurped at a bite of sandwich. Two-twenty-four meant this place was only two blocks from the river. Unless it was in one of the rehabbed zones close to the river, it was in a pretty bad area, and somehow the idea of rooming houses didn't fit into rehab programs.

"I guess you had to use all my money to find this out?"

He gave me a toothy grin. "Knowledge takes money, my dear."

"Am I paying for that sandwich?"

"There are some questions that are not appropriate to ask of a gentleman."

"Is it appropriate to screw a woman and not get her pants off?"

He laughed. "Some things do work better one way than another."

I started to ask him another question but noticed a reflection in the window of the restaurant. A car parked across the street looked like the car that I saw behind me when I left Bolinski's apartment. I couldn't see the faces of the people inside, but it looked like two men. "Condie."

"Yes, my dear."

"See that old grey Chevy parked across the street?"

"Yeah, kind of tacky, isn't it?"

"Can you tell me what the guys inside look like?" I was keeping my back to the street and using Condie's eyes.

He laid his sandwich on his plate. "Someone tailing you, my dear?"

"Maybe."

"Want me to have them taken care of?"

"No! What I need to know is why they're following me. Just tell me what they look like."

"Sorry, dearie, I can't see much. Too dark in there."

"Tell you what. I'm gonna leave. Watch them to see if they leave when I do. Try to get a license number if you can. Okay?"

"After you bought me this lovely sandwich, certainly."

I gave him half a dirty look and walked down the block to my car. The grey Chevy didn't waste much time in following me once I was out on the street. I didn't want to go anyplace they may be interested in, so I drove straight out to I-70 and headed west. I was making no attempt to speed or do anything to lose them. I called Condie on my cell.

"Could only get the first three numbers," he said.

"They were going too fast for the last three letters."

"Thanks. That might help." Now I had to figure out where I was going. I really didn't want the guys behind me to know I knew they were following me. I really wanted to know who they were and *why* they were following me. I finally took an exit ramp, looking for someplace to stop. I pulled into a gas station and gassed up the car. Looking out of the corner of my eyes, I watched the grey Chevy go past. Maybe they weren't following me. Maybe they just got tired of the game for the day, but that didn't seem plausible.

Before I headed back into the city, I checked my watch. It was Smitty's time. When I walked in the door, Tony Marsalis was sitting at the bar, and Kenny was coming from the jukebox saying something about knowing when to hold 'em and knowing when to fold 'em. Try to figure out whether to hold or fold didn't sound like as much fun as dealing with Tony, so guess who won?

I ate a burger and fries because I hadn't had any lunch. Then Tony and I started on long necks. Not long after that, we danced while Ray sang about Georgia on his mind. Then one long neck led to another, and the next thing I really remembered was waking up in Tony's bed about ten the next morning. I had to lay there for awhile, thinking about what caused me to end up there and what happened *after* we got there. That part brought a smile to my face. I started remembering the "what happened" part.

Tony had already gone to work, so I wobbled into his shower and stood underneath a hot spray of water for about fifteen minutes. Then it was a treasure hunt to find all my clothing. When I accomplished that chore, I got a cup of coffee he left in the pot for me. I sat at the kitchen table and thought about what I needed to do for the day. The first part of my plan involved going back to my place, changing clothes, and picking up my Glock. I liked to have that with me anytime I was going into a known "rough" area.

The area I ended up in would not have been shown on

a Chamber of Commerce brochure. I checked my rear view mirror all the way down there, but no grey Chevy. I thought I saw a small white car a few times, but there are thousands of them in St. Louis. Nothing to get excited about. I parked right in front of the building I was looking for. There were very few cars on the street, but I figured most of the people who lived around there couldn't afford them. About half the cars there were on blocks.

There was a sign in the window of the place advertising "Room for Let." A woman with gigantic wrinkles in her forehead and chin opened the door for me. She reminded me of one of those cartoons where if you turned the picture upside down, the person would be smiling, but I had no chance to turn her over to see. I just had to put up with her frown.

"Is Norm Bolinski here?" I asked politely.

"No one here by that name," she answered and started to close the door.

I got my foot in before she got a chance to complete the process. I showed her a picture. "How about this guy?"

She took the picture and moved it back and forth several times until she had it in her focal range. "That's Nick Bronco." She gave me a squinty look. "You the law?"

"Private. So he's here?"

"Probably still in bed. Sleeps most of the day." She stepped back and let me in. "First door on the left up the stairs. Ain't gonna be no trouble, is there? You'll have to pay for any damages."

"I just need to deliver a message to him." Actually, I just wanted to make sure it was the same guy. All I was paid to do was find him—nothing more.

I knocked softy on the door then leaned over slightly to put my ear up to it to listen. I heard a gruff voice from inside. "Who the hell's there?"

"My name's Meg Bartlett. I'd like to talk to you."

"What about?"

"Are you Norm Bolinski?"

Then two things happened at once. I heard glass

breaking downstairs, and a shot was fired from the other side of the door where I was listening. The slug passed a couple of inches in front of my face, and I felt an immediate pain in my nose. I may have heard another shot coming from downstairs. My ears were ringing by that time. Then someone was running up the steps. I ducked down the hall and into a small alcove. I drew my Glock. I couldn't see what was going on, but I heard what sounded like a door being kicked open. Then two shots. Someone was rattling around in Nick Bronco's room. I stepped from the alcove and levelled my Glock down the hallway. Jake Cash stepped from the room, carrying a suitcase. A complete picture of what had happened flashed in my mind. Jake couldn't find the guy he was looking for, so he hired me to do it. Then he followed me, little white car and all, so he could kill the guy and steal a suitcase. In short, he simply used me!

"Hold it, Jake!"

He had already put his pistol back in the waistband of his pants, but he went for it. I fired two shots. Jake fell backwards down the steps, hit the suitcase on the banister, and money was suddenly floating around like confetti. I walked over to the edge of the steps to make sure he wasn't moving. I opened my cell and called 911 and then Mel Kirkland.

Norm and Jake were both dead. The landlady apparently tried to stop Jake from coming in, so he just broke a door glass and shot her. She was still alive. I got a chance to look at her while she was on the floor. Her face was upside down, but she still wasn't smiling. The paramedics pulled a large splinter from my nose. Then they covered the small hole with a humongous bandage. I looked like I'd had a face transplant.

It turned out Jake, Norm, and a couple of other guys had robbed a Brink's truck in Kansas City. Somehow, Norm managed to get away with all of the loot. Jake had heard he was around St. Louis, so he came in, rented an apartment, made up the story about the wife, hired me, and just followed me around until I located the two million for him. Being used has never made me happy.

Getting a reward from Brinks for the return of their money made me very happy.

SING TO ME

Everett C. Gavel, Jr.

Sing to me,
my sultry raven,
Let me hear you melt the rocks nearby,
Make this place, this moment,
my momentary haven.
Sing like you can make the angels fly!
Your voice is a gift,
A glorious gift from god,
Being in love with another, and hearing you,
always makes my heart feel odd!
But sing, sing, sing like you can!
Make our ears orgasm,
and everyone within range,
a lifelong, emotion-filled fan!
Please, my raven,
please sing to me again,
Then I must go,
and try to explain where I've been.

SIMPLY IRRESISTIBLE

Betty Dobson

"I can't wear sleeveless," I said, tossing another dress over the dressing room door. "My arms are too flabby."

Antonia fired back a stream of Italian curses and three more wardrobe selections. "Try the red one. You look great in red."

"Maybe," I said, draping the velvety dress in front of me and staring into the mirror. "But it looks awful clingy. My belly . . ."

"Santa Madonna!" Antonia's face appeared over the door. "I should have such a belly. In Italy, you would be a goddess."

I dropped the dress and spread my arms as I glared up at her. "Yeah? Well, this is Nova Scotia, my dear. Men around here don't even believe in goddesses until they see someone like you."

"Listen, girl." Antonia rattled the door. "Put on the damn dress. Come on, please? Just try it." She vanished with a squeal and a thump.

"Are you okay?"

"Never mind me. How's the dress?"

"Hang on." I leaned into the mirror and whispered, "Bitch."

"That just means you know I'm right." Three raps on the door. "Hurry up. I want to see."

I barely had the door unlatched when she grabbed my hand and dragged me to the mirror. I almost tripped over an overturned chair, but Antonia didn't miss a beat.

The store clerk poked her head into the dressing area and gave us her best retail smile. "Can I help you ladies with anything?"

Antonia pointed to the ceiling and cocked her head. "Yes, I think you can. Come here," she said, pulling the clerk in to stand beside me. "Look at this woman. Doesn't she look beautiful in this dress? Tell her how beautiful she looks."

The clerk leaned back and squinted. "It really is a lovely dress."

"Frig the dress." Antonia dragged me past the clerk and into the store. "Are there any men in here?"

A volley of plain English profanity ricocheted inside my head. The dressing room exuded a magnetic pull. A powerful force of nature, but no match for Antonia on a mission. I tried to keep my eyes turned down but got distracted by the deep flush rising from my low neckline. Like a glass filling with red wine. For this, she would have to die.

"Now, tell me she's not gorgeous." Antonia had her arm draped over the shoulders of a man in denim and green plaid. She leaned into him as if whispering tart nothings.

"I don't know." He stared at the ceiling and fidgeted with his belt buckle. "I'm just here with my girlfriend."

"I'm not asking her. I want to know what you think. Take a good look."

"Enough." The word spilled out of me just as the burning blush reached my throat. "Let the poor guy go. I'll take the dress."

Antonia lowered her eyes and spoke softly. "Well, don't do it unless you want to. I'm only making a suggestion."

I almost believed her, until she flicked me a look through black lashes and smiled like a well-fed rat. "Don't you ever get tired of winning?"

"Of course not. But I also lose, you know."

I did know. And I felt like crap for reminding her.

"Never mind," she said. "I feel like dancing now. Pay for the dress and let's go."

"Give me a minute to change."

"No, just pay. I'll get your things."

"I am not going to the bar looking like this."

"And what better time? I know you, Tammy. You'll hang the dress in the back of your closet and pretend that owning it is bold enough. No. You will wear it tonight." With a backwards wave, she disappeared into the dressing room.

The cashier dodged my tight smile as I passed her my credit card. The machine soon made a happy noise. As I signed the slip, she pulled a tiny pair of scissors from under the counter. "I can cut the tag off if you like. Wouldn't want you to be embarrassed."

She had no idea. As much as I admired Antonia's confidence and vitality, I wished she would tone it down sometimes.

How good it felt, though, to know she existed just beyond familiarity and to dip into her world from time to time.

The scissors snipped behind my ear. "You're all set. Oh, and we have a no return policy on sale items. Have a nice evening."

Good thing she'd already put the scissors away. I felt positively homicidal.

My mood hadn't improved much by the time we reached the bar. Chris Perkins, local letch about town, finished the job, fulfilling my worst fears.

"Hey Tammy," Chris said, pinning me to the bar. "Wicked dress. Don't have to wonder what you'd look like out of it. Can I buy you a draft?"

"No thanks," I said. "Gives me a headache. Is Julie here yet?"

"Back playing pool. Listen, I'd be willing to spring for a bar shot." He brushed his fingers along my shoulder. "Really nice dress."

"Yeah, well, there's plenty left at Walmart, but I don't think they carry your size."

He threw his hands up. "Hey, you know me, Tammy. Just pulling your leg."

Antonia slipped between us, somehow, and batted her eyes at Chris. "Well, it's certainly obvious you wanted to pull something. Why don't you go hit on someone who doesn't know you? I think that works better for you."

"Figures," Chris said, looking around with a smirk. "Come to defend your girlfriend?"

"It's true. You could turn a woman gay. But first she would have to care." Antonia put her arm around my waist. "So you see, we are quite unaffected. But I see by the bulge in your pants that you are not. Is this some sort of fantasy you have?"

Chris just sort of melted away, though I thought I heard him mutter something about the can.

Catching the bartender's eye was easy at that point. I ordered two Blues and passed one to Antonia. "I could have handled him."

"And you were. But I wanted to have some fun, too."

"That wasn't fun."

"Then why did you not stop me?"

I took a mouthful of beer and let it go down slowly. "You can be a little overpowering. I don't like to get in your way."

"Oh, such bullshit." She really did like the feel of English profanity on her tongue. "You're a woman, not a girl. Not even I can tell you what to do."

"Then why do you try?"

"Come over here," she said, pointing to a corner far from the bar. "People listen too much. Yes, I am talking about you." She wagged her finger at William Polanski, who quickly turned away.

"Suddenly you want privacy." I stomped to the corner and plunked myself into a chair. "So, what's the awful truth?"

"My friend, you do not know what you want until someone shows you. No, I'm not done. Whatever you will be, I can't decide that. I can only show you possibilities. Take what you like. Throw away the rest. I won't be offended." She sat down across from me and rested her elbows on the table. "Now, talk. Tell me what you think."

"I think you're a bitch," I said. "But that's a compliment in my family."

"So it does mean I'm right."

"It means I understand your motives, but your methods suck. I don't need to catch a pie in the face to know that whipped cream tastes good."

"Now you're making me hungry."

I had to laugh. Much as I didn't want to, I had no choice. "Pie's too fattening."

"Not if I'm going to have a beautiful belly like yours."

"And just then," I said, hands splayed over my heart, "the man of my dreams walked through the door. Or was it a flying pig?" Another round of laughter stuck in my throat. The man at the door—really at the door—would never pass for anyone's dream.

Antonia kept laughing. I didn't have the heart to stop her. But she must have seen something in my face. Like maybe the snarl I couldn't suppress.

"What's going on?"

"Rick's here."

Antonia seemed to fold in on herself. Rick always had that effect—her own immovable object.

The piped in music owned the air. No voices. Everyone there—all the regulars, at least—knew about Rick. They knew what he did to Antonia and what it took for her to finally leave him. Only Rick didn't handle rejection very well.

"I just want to talk to her."

"You're not supposed to be here, Poole." Chris stood in Rick's path, effectively blocking his view—at least for the moment.

William swivelled his stool away from the bar. Hands clasped between his knees, he spoke in a low, firm voice. "Go home, Rick. Don't burn your last chance."

"I just want to talk to her."

"Maybe so, but she doesn't want to talk to you." Chris' bravado surprised me. He'd never shown much character before.

Antonia's lips moved, so slightly that I thought she might cry. But then I could see words forming, silent and hollow, each one a chink in her resolve.

"Antonia, no." I grabbed both her hands in mine. "Come on, it can't be this easy for him to get to you. Not anymore."

"Get me out of here." Her words barely rippled the air between us.

I looked around. Both exits lay at Rick's end of the bar. But we could still reach the fire door, out behind the pool tables—so long as we could get around the corner without him seeing her.

The air cracked. Sounded like a cue ball slamming into an eight. White on black. Only louder. Sharper. And echoed in a woman's scream.

I hit the floor hard. Something wet against my cheek. Oh God! I could feel the weight of Antonia's body. Hear the rattle of distant voices.

"Are you hurt?"

I opened one eye to Antonia's fuzzy profile. Not dead. "Fine. I think. Were you hit?"

"No," she whispered. Then she rolled off me, into the shadow of the pool table. She crouched low, craning her neck to see beyond the thick table leg. "Is he gone? Can you see?"

I saw the huddled forms of people hiding behind the table. Good for them.

Black shoes blocked my view. I'd have to move to see a face. What the hell. Figured Rick would shoot either way.

"Come on, get up."

Okay, that wasn't Rick's voice. I flopped over with a heavy sigh and smiled up at Chris with uncustomary sincerity. "Did he really have a gun?"

"Oh yeah. I think William's making him eat it."

Antonia darted out and up. "Where is he?" She flew toward the bar, trailing black curls in her wake. "Where is the son of a bitch?"

Chris scratched his head. "So much for terrified. Maybe we should have gotten Rick to safety first."

"Wouldn't work," I said, smoothing down my new

dress. "Does that look like a beer stain to you?"

"Don't know. Let me smell."

I blocked his face with the palm of my hand. "Never mind."

Antonia came bouncing back, a satisfied grin wound across her face. "Let's go somewhere else."

"Sure," Chris said. "Look, I can drive you home."

"Frig that." Antonia hugged me and kissed my wet cheek. "You smell like beer, my sweet. We want to catch men, not flies. Come wash that off. Then we go to the Dome."

"Hang on," I said, hands in the air. "Bad enough wearing this dress in front of friends. But strangers?"

"Are you still worried about that? Unbelievable."

"Well, let's not forget I'm broke."

"No problem." She reached into her purse and pulled out a thick black wallet. "I'm thinking Rick won't need this in jail."

FEMME BRUTALE
Gretchen Wilsenach

The rain was pouring steadily—not unusual for Paris in April.

On the spur of the moment, Sandrine ducked into the Internet café. It was as good a time as any to check if that e-mail had arrived yet.

As she waited for her allotted booth to be vacated, she glanced over at the monitor in the adjoining booth, realizing immediately that its occupant was engrossed in an online chat room conversation. Squinting a little, Sandrine tried to make out the nick he was using and rolled her eyes when she saw that he wanted to be known in the cyber world as "casanova123." She chuckled inwardly at the choice of persona—*Ten for conceit, zilch for originality,* she thought as she slipped into her seat and expertly opened the website of her Internet provider.

Sandrine let out a little "yeah" when she read the e-mail that confirmed she got the job to shoot a well-known fashion model for a magazine.

With a victorious smile on her face, she left the seat almost at the exact instant as the world's greatest lover left his. They both apologized as they bumped into each other and left the Internet café and stepped out into the deluge.

The coffee aroma was never more inviting than at the little bistro on the corner of Rue de Beaux, and Sandrine entered without hesitating. There was one free table, and she got to it at the same time as another customer whom she immediately recognized as the Casanova with the numbers.

"Why don't we share?" he asked.

"Why don't we?"

They both ordered coffee, hers was café au lait, and his was espresso.

When Sandrine took her diary from her bag and began

scribbling notes into it, Casanova took his mobile from his pocket and began sending someone an SMS message. It was as if the silence between them was forced, awkward.

Their coffees arrived, and as she reached for the sugar, so did he. Their hands collided, and for the first time they actually looked at each other. Sandrine noticed his eyelashes first, long and black, nice chin and nose, and a very sexy mouth. So perhaps he was as real a Casanova as the historical playboy whose name he had borrowed, she mused.

"Is something bothering you?" he asked.

"Not at all. Why do you ask?"

"The way you looked at me made me think you are mad at me."

"Not at all, in fact I am very happy right now and nothing can upset my feeling of contentment."

"My name is Joe. What's yours?"

"Joe? You don't look like a 'Joe' at all. I am Sandrine."

He laughed aloud. "What does a 'Joe' normally look like then?"

"American, I would say."

"You do have a point. It's a nickname only, for Joseph. I am of Mid-Eastern origin." He took a pack of Gauloise from his pocket and offered her one. Sandrine accepted, wishing for the second time that day that she could break the habit. She coughed and crushed the cigarette in the ashtray.

They started chatting, and before long they were telling each other silly little things, like what they would most like to do on a rainy day in Paris.

Joe said he would like to be in bed with a nice lady. (Of course this was what she expected he would say but did not let him know she knew of his vainglorious *amour-propre*.)

"I would love to be on a train going somewhere, maybe the TGV, speeding fast over pretty landscapes, watching little villages pass by my window."

"You sound like a romantic."

"And you sound like a would-be Casanova," Sandrine replied as innocently as she could.

He did not blink. They drank their coffee in silence and smoked, blowing twirls of white furls into the already smoky bistro.

"Let's take the TGV somewhere."

She looked at him as if he was crazy.

"You are insane." She giggled slightly.

"Why? One of us should at least get their wish fulfilled. Let's go to the *Gare* and see which TGV leaves first, we take it . . . have lunch at our destination then come back. Unless you have something better to do." His eyes challenged her.

"*D'accord.*" She did not have anything better to do, and she had so much to feel happy about at that moment. Let her celebrate the day in this unusual way, she thought.

Joe paid for the coffee, and they left the bistro. He hailed a taxi and told the driver to take them to the *Gare de Lyon*.

Thirty minutes later, they were facing each other over yet another small table, this time in a speeding TGV heading for Lyon.

She smiled like a happy child. He looked at her, fascinated and surprised that she accepted the challenge, intrigued by her special beauty of which she seemed unaware.

Sandrine wondered what on earth made her do this crazy thing, accepting to go to Lyon with a total stranger. Was it because he was extraordinarily handsome? He was evidently aware of this fact.

They drank some tea on the train and looked through the window, enjoying the speed of the train . . . at the little houses rushing by in misty rain. They smiled a lot but did not talk much, each busy with their own thoughts.

When they finally arrived at Lyon, she asked if they were boarding the return train back immediately.

"Let's have lunch first. It would be a mortal sin to be in Lyon and pass the cuisine by. I know a little place that is owned by a woman chef. We need a taxi."

Sandrine's eyes lit up with anticipation.

The little restaurant turned out to be a world famous one, and they were lucky to be given a table. Lunch was an unforgettable experience. Joe seemed to know how to order the right food with the right wine. He offered her champagne, but she refused, insisting that the wine was delicious enough. The ambiance soon made them relax with each other, and by the end of the meal they were laughing, making fun of each other and telling silly jokes. They laughed till tears ran down their faces. A better time was not had by either one of them in years. They did not, however, divulge their past or present situations to each other, but it did not seem to matter to either one.

When they finally left the restaurant, it was late in the afternoon and raining in Lyon as it had been raining in Paris. They took a taxi to the station only to discover that they had just missed the train to Paris. They looked at each other for a long, long time without saying anything . . . until finally . . .

"Shall we find a hotel?" His question implied everything she expected. She nodded.

When they finally found themselves back on the train the next day, speeding towards Paris, Joe was sitting next to her this time, holding her hand intimately.

She leaned into him, watching villages perched on top of hills in the distance. The sun was shining. There was not that much to say. They had said it all the night before. In words and in silence. In actions.

When they arrived at the *Gare de Lyon*, he offered to take her to wherever she was staying.

"No Joe, I will take my own taxi from here. There are some things I have to get on my way home. Thank you for a wonderful adventure." She reached over on her toes and kissed him softly on his cheek. He bent and kissed her on both cheeks, then on her forehead, then on the palm of her hand.

"I will call you."

How, she wondered? He never asked for her telephone number. She stepped into the waiting taxi and never looked back once. Tears began to flow down her cheeks in unstoppable streams.

Sandrine threw herself into her work with ardent energy. They were shooting at different locations in Paris, which was not always the easiest way to shoot for an out-of-town photographer who ached for her own studio with controlled light.

The model was incredible, looking ordinary when she arrived; what happened in front of the camera was amazing. Sandrine had never worked with a more photogenic face than this before. The shoot was a feast. Everybody was ecstatic.

Sandrine needed to do some work on the photographs to achieve special effects that the client wanted. The three-day shoot was over, and she could return home to London soon. She was offered the apartment for a month while pre-production and the shoot were on. She loved the thrill of living in Paris like a real Parisian. Her French was impeccable, so people mistakenly thought she was French. She loved that, too.

Later, when she sat in front of her Apple, her thoughts started flipping back to her day with Joe. It was a most amazing day, one she would always remember. What she could not understand or accept, though, was why he had made no effort to stay in touch with her.

He did not ask for her address or her telephone number. Nothing. A kiss on the hand, and that was that.

She checked her e-mail and answered the ones she had to attend to. More shoots were lined up for her in London and one in Madrid. "Yeah," she said out loud. Then her mind started taking her back to the day in the Internet café. "casanova123." That was easy to remember.

How many different chat messengers could there be? Yahoo!, MSN, and IM were the ones she knew. She downloaded all three onto her laptop. Then she created her own cyber identity. She nicknamed herself "La Mysterieuse," and soon she was in another world, searching for a nickname that would be recognized and accepted. Casanova123! Her heart jumped when suddenly on Yahoo! Messenger the name appeared. She did not know what to do. She did not have long to wait before the name sent her a message.

> **Casanova123:** Hi! Do I know u? You asked to be on my list

> **La Mysterieuse:** I think I made a mistake in the numbers, are you Johnny?"

> **Casanova123:** No, not – but if u are nice and pretty u can stay on my list, hahaha

Is that right? she thought, and suddenly she was mad with fury.

> **La Mysterieuse:** Most people think I'm okay. Not too bad, I mean.

> **Casanova123:** Can I see your pic?

How damn impertinent. Maybe it was time somebody put him in his rightful place.

> **La Mysterieuse:** I have so many pictures, but I don't know how to show it to you.

He explained how she could send him a photograph via the messenger. She asked for a few minutes to find one. Deftly, she picked one of the shots she had taken earlier that day then pulled it into Photoshop and made a few alterations to the colour and light. It was quite a sexy photograph. There was the model posing with her head to the side, the gown was strapless and backless in white satin, exposing soft white skin. Sandrine changed the hue to an intense blue, which automatically changed the colour of the eyes and hair as well. She bit her lip nervously. She sent the file containing the photograph, and her heart beat wildly with excitement and fear at the deceitful thing she was doing.

Casanova123: Is this YOU?

La Mysterieuse: Yes.

Casanova123: You are beautiful

La Mysterieuse: I have to be, I'm a model.

Casanova123: Really?

La Mysterieuse: Sure.

Casanova123: When can I neet you?

She waited.

Casanova123: Sorry that was meant to be MEET hahaha

La Mysterieuse: Well first you have to yell me where you live.

La Mysterieuse: (Aw man! Your typos are contagious! I meant TELL - hihi)

Casanova123: In Paris. You?

La Mysterieuse: I'm in Tokyo now, I was in Paris a dew days ago.

Casanova123: What u doing in Tokyo?

La Mysterieuse: I told you, I'm a model - I go where I am needed.

Casanova123: I really want to need you. When will you be back in Paris?

With the message, he sent a smiling face emoticon. Oh yes, she still remembered his "needs."

La Mysterieuse: Excuse me?

Casanova123: That was another typo. No offence!

La Mysterieuse: I'm not sure, I may have to go to NY soon. Can I see your photo now?

Casanova123: Ok hold on

Soon she saw a file heading towards her laptop. Once again her heart was beating so fast she could hardly breathe. She opened the file . . . and there was Joe's face, looking at her, grinning like a Cheshire cat. The rat!

La Mysterieuse: You are very handsome, you could be a model too. What do you do?

Casanova123: Nothing as exciting as you. I'm a maitre d' at a restaurant in Paris

So, that was why he was so knowledgeable about food and wine when he took her to lunch on that fateful day.

La Mysterieuse: Well it was nice talking to you, see you again, I have to go.

Casanova123: No please stay, please

La Mysterieuse: Sorry I have to go now. Bye.

Casanova123: Wait! Wait! Can I e-mail you?

La Mysterieuse: You can see my e-mail here - so feel free.

Sandrine hoped her answer sounded nonchalant.

La Mysterieuse: Bye.

Casanova123: Wait...whats your name?

La Mysterieuse: hahahahaa

She logged off and sighed. She hoped that would make him suffer a bit. Seeing that beautiful woman with the long exposed neck. May he suffer in hell. She took a shower and slipped into bed. But sleep escaped her for many hours. Her thoughts kept going back to that one night in Lyon. It was everything she had ever wanted a romantic night to be. He was amazingly tender and loving, it was so easy to love him. The bastard!

Sandrine was not surprised to find an e-mail waiting for her the next day. He asked her what time she would be able to log onto Yahoo! Messenger again. She had to find out the time difference between Tokyo and Paris; she did this and made a mental note of it. She was thinking he used an Internet café, which meant he did not have a computer at home. She worked out an impossible time and wrote back suggesting that they meet again at a time he was sure to be working.

Joe returned her mail with a pleading request for her to make another time; he was working on that day. He made an alternative suggestion. Sandrine of course rejected that, saying she would be at a shoot then.

Then he asked for her telephone number.

She answered that she did not have "roving" on her mobile phone.

Joe asked if she could call him and sent her his telephone number at home as well as his mobile number. *Merde!* It took a pretty face to get him supplying contacts, did it?

She considered leaving things just there. This was enough already. Talking to him hurt. Bastard! Sandrine left her apartment and walked the streets. Then she saw a hair salon she had meant to go to for ages and always put it off. Now was the time. She had an urge to change her looks, the colour of her hair, the style.

A few hours later, a new Sandrine walked out of the salon, highlights in her now reddish hair. She took the Metro to Galleries Lafayette and splurged on new make-up. Maybe she underplayed her looks a bit, and it was time to accentuate a bit more.

When Sandrine met the agent for dinner that same evening to hand over the discs, she was complimented on her new look. She felt good. What if this was the restaurant that Joe worked at? She paled at the very thought. She would not be able to handle the situation.

And then her worst fear came into play; she saw him talking to some people. He was all dressed in suit and tie. He looked handsome and elegant. She ducked her head sideways so he would not see her. Her agent, Pierre, talked non-stop and booked her for another shoot. She hardly heard a word he was saying, only that it was for a well-known cosmetic house.

"Monsieur, Madame, may I offer you some champagne that we have on promotion tonight?" She recognized his voice instantly and again almost fainted. Then he looked at her, and his face changed colour. He almost spilled the champagne as he poured. She said nothing. She pretended not to know him. But she knew that he knew she knew.

The rest of the evening was a blur to her. They left without so much as another sight of Joe.

When Sandrine got home, she immediately logged on. There was an e-mail waiting for her.

"Please, please," he begged, wouldn't she make some effort to meet him again on Yahoo! Messenger? He was eager to speak to her; she had put a spell on him.

She opened her Yahoo! and found messages jumping onto her screen. She left him a message:

> **La Mysterieuse:** Hi Casanova, I was waiting here for hours, but you never showed up. I guess you are busy. Take care till we meet again.

Sandrine left for London the following day. When she entered her flat, she was met by a zillion pieces of mail, put on her desk by the cleaning lady who came to clean for her once a week. She sifted through them and threw them down . . . she was more interested in her "other" mail. When she opened her mailbox, there were no less than seven e-mails from Joe. She opened Yahoo! and again messages from him flew onto her screen. Suddenly she didn't feel so good about the whole vengeful attack she had launched against him. She realized that she was looking forward to his e-mails, that she missed him. She still played out the night in Lyon in her fantasies. She hurt.

Then "he" appeared on her screen, and she almost jumped off her chair.

> **Casanova123:** There u are, at last, oh my God I have missd you so much. When are you coming back?

She had almost forgotten that she was supposed to be in Tokyo.

> **La Mysterieuse:** Soon. Very soon. The shoot is almost done.

> **Casanova123:** Will u be able to come to Paris? Please say YES!

> **La Mysterieuse:** I will do my best. I really don't know.

This was not going the way she had wanted it to go.

> **Casanova123:** We have to meet. I have set my mind on meeting u...please baby - don't let me die and suffer like this

> **La Mysterieuse:** Of course I won't make you suffer. Why should I do that? But tell me, have you ever made anybody suffer?

> **Casanova123:** That's a strange question - but to be honest - I don't know - I hope not. I don't like to hurt people.

> **La Mysterieuse:** Wow! What a sweet person you are. You have never intentionally hurt anybody. That's great to know. So I can be assured that you will never hurt me?

> **Casanova123:** Never, I will die before I hurt you

> **La Mysterieuse:** WOW, and all those promises just because I have a pretty face? How can I be sure you won't get bored with me?

> **Casanova123:** I have forgotten what u look like ages ago. I love u for yoursefl now. You are a sweet wonderful girl, your tenderness speaks to me all the time.

> **La Mysterieuse:** Are you telling the truth?

He was some liar. Such a convincing liar. Damn.

> **La Mysterieuse**: You know that I am falling in love with you...don't you?

She shook as she typed the words. What was she doing? She would be getting herself into something deeper than she had imagined. Deep shit for sure. But she could not help herself.

> **Casanova123:** You are making me the happiest man in the world. I dream of the day I can make love to you, for real. In fact, I want to take you home to meet my parents.
>
> **La Mysterieuse:** You are soooooooooooo crazy hahahaha

She laughed aloud.

They talked for almost an hour. Not about lies, but about his family, where he grew up and about his school days. How his father wanted him to follow him into the business back home. But he thought he was wiser and needed to get away, to "sow his oats," he said. She asked him if being a glorified waiter made his father happy.

> **Casanova123:** I have not spoken to my father since I left. He has disowned me. But I know that if I go back and go into the business, everything will be ok again. Will you go with me? Could you live in my country as my wife?
>
> **La Mysterieuse:** You are out of your mind.
>
> **Casanova123:** I am asking you to marry me. I mean it. From my heart.
>
> **La Mysterieuse:** Joe, I am honoured, thank you, but the answer is NO! I can't!

Oh shit, she called him "Joe" without thinking. She cringed, hoping he would not pick up the faux pas.

> **Casanova123:** Why? You don't want to pose for cameras all your life do you?

Sandrine was thinking fast. How did she get out of this dilemma? Things had gone far enough. She had to stop it.

> **La Mysterieuse:** I don't know how to tell you, but I am already married.

It seemed like an eternity had passed. He did not respond.

> **La Mysterieuse:** Are you there? *Gone na sai!*

She had just told him she was sorry in Japanese.

> **Casanova123:** You just said you were falling for me - I believe that you are in love with me. I can feel it. Meet me. Just meet me. Once we meet you can decide if you want to stay with your husband or not. I swear I will be good to you. I am crying now.
>
> **La Mysterieuse:** I am crying too. I am truly sorry. But now I have to go. I will mail you tomorrow. Sorry – and…I love you!

She logged off before he could respond to her. That hurt. She told him only one real truth. That she loved him.

The days passed, and as Joe's e-mails arrived in her mailbox, she deleted them without reading. She cried for days, and then she got up and took a walk in the park. Sandrine organized her next shoots and went to pre-prod meetings. She kept herself as busy as she could and filled her mind with more stuff than she could cope with. It helped to a certain degree.

One week after she had spoken to Joe, she opened his last imploring e-mail. She read it as tears filled her eyes and made a decision.

To: casanova123@yahoo.fr
From: londonrain@yahoo.uk
Date: April 25, 2004

Dear Casanova,

My friend told me all about you. I am sorry to be the one to tell you, but she is dead.

Her husband found your mails and in a fit of jealousy he slit her throat. He is Japanese and his anger knew no bounds. A mutual friend of ours called me to tell me. I am so sorry. I hope you can continue your life without too much regrets and sorrow.

I wish you all the best.
Madeleine.

She clicked Send . . . and sat back in her chair.

What else could she do but kill the woman who stole her Joe's heart?

RESISTANCE
Betty Dobson

Mother Hildegard broke the news in the middle of morning supplication. Perimeter cameras had detected unusual shrub traffic outside the north wall. Even Penelope, the order's youngest novitiate, understood the significance. Head bowed and hands clasped, she shuffled to her post.

Uncertainty expressed itself in sweat. Rivulets formed beneath her stiff habit. Penelope knew how to shoot, but she'd never had to fire on a live target before. But she would honour her sacred vow. The Sisters of Perpetual Resistance could rely on no one but themselves.

Sister Constance had already taken up position, hunched over the range finder. "Two minutes, Novitiate. Twelve seconds too slow."

"Apologies, Sister. I took a wrong turn in the vestibule."

"Sit." Sister Constance flapped one beefy hand towards the corner console. "And pray you get the chance to improve your response time."

The wall exploded inward. Shattered stone flew like hail amid the lightning strikes of the enemy's electrical cannon. Sister Constance, knocked unconscious by the first blast, died quietly when the second volley toppled the range finder.

Penelope watched through cloudy veil and unblinking eyes. The Lore Books spoke of such carnage. Temples demolished. Sisters killed, and they the lucky ones.

Gunfire echoed through the corridors. No longer at the gates, the enemy had breached the sanctuary.

Penelope gripped her breasts and whispered to the air. "Great Mother, bless this vessel, untouched by any hands but mine. Nurture these hands that they may strike true. I defend you unto death, that I may look upon your radiant face."

The click of a rifle bolt punctuated Penelope's rites. A lone trooper rounded the corner, his face obscured by a visoured helmet, his lean frame sheathed in ultra-light armour. He turned his head every which way but kept his muzzle focused on Penelope.

"Take off that veil. I want to see your face."

Penelope kept her hands clasped under her apron, drawing some comfort from the cold metal of her hidden derringer.

"Take it off, or I will." He raised the rifle to eye level. "Dead or alive, your face'll look the same."

"No doubt," Penelope said, rolling the veil up and over. "Just as the reward credits will carry the same weight."

The trooper took a step back and let the rifle fall against his leg. "Penny?"

"I am called Penelope within these walls."

"Penny, it's me. Josh." He pulled off his helmet, revealing a tumble of blond hair. "What're you doing here?"

"Restoring my soul. If only you could say the same."

"No such thing," Josh said, taking three small steps forward. "You can't live your life according to some outdated mythology."

"You don't belong here." Penelope drew the derringer, slowly bringing it level with Josh's Adam's apple.

He snapped the rifle into firing position. The barrel paralleled her arm. "Are you trying to get yourself killed?"

Distant shots echoed all around them. Closer at hand, a stifled cry drifted from the garden.

"If I have the choice," she said. "If you're the man I remember."

Josh caressed the trigger's soft inner curve. He knew the rules. Penny's disorder made her a danger to society. The law demanded death or humiliation. "It won't be that bad, Penny. You always did worry too much over such a simple act. And when it's over, you can go back to your real life. We can still get married."

Penelope shook her head. "You don't understand.

Penny died three months ago. That life doesn't exist anymore." She lowered the derringer and sank to her knees in one fluid motion. "Come pray with me."

Josh angled the rifle downward, drawing a deep breath. "Stop it. You don't really believe this stuff."

"I can believe nothing else." She brought her hands together, cradling the derringer.

"You have to come with me."

"One last prayer, and I'll go." Eyes closed and head bowed, she whispered the words of devotion. Her hands moved in tandem with the words, a pentacle drawn on air. From the lips to the left breast, up to the right shoulder and across to the opposite, down to the right breast and back to the lips. She kissed her thumbs, brushing cold metal.

"Okay. Enough." Josh lowered the rifle and held out his free hand. "Let's go."

"Go with love, Joshua." She kissed the derringer, lips parted as if for a lover.

Josh fell to his knees, his rifle untouched by his side. Heavy footfalls drew nearer with each clouded blink. He hadn't done his job, but he could still do his duty. He kissed the back of her left hand three times and slid her abandoned solitaire onto the third finger.

"Go with love," he whispered. "If only I could do the same."

MAESTRO
Gretchen Wilsenach

The theatre was packed to capacity with *Portenos,* known to be as intensely passionate about their music as they were of life itself. The Teatro Colon in Buenos Aires is on par with such celebrated theatres as the La Scala in Milan and the Opera in Paris, the productions world class. Tonight was no different, and some of the crowd came from beyond the Rio de la Plata to attend this wondrous celebration of their very own kinsman, the talented and still single-at-forty-seven Alejandro Mañues. The long awaited première of his new work, the "Gypsy Concerto," was to be conducted that night under the baton of the maestro himself.

It was a well-known fact that most of the women who came to his performances were there to look only at him, that instead of discriminating ears, they possessed other senses of heightened interest. With his almost shoulder-length black hair and fine Latin features, he was every mature female's idea of heaven.

There was an audible quietude inside the compressed seating, from the back rows to the gilded galleries. Everybody gasped for breath when the first musicians came onto the stage and took their places. The first violinist stood and played a few repeated A tones for the others to tune their instruments. Some few, final, momentary coughs and chair shuffling permeated, then came the total stillness of respect.

Alejandro walked onto the stage, fast-dressed in tight, black pants that almost resembled a toreador's, with a white, gipsy shirt. His baton, reputed to be privately expensed, pure Narwhal ivory, was golden-handled and saved for his most dramatic performances. Tonight, the audience recognized that glimmer in his hand.

The eager listeners stood up and clapped as he bowed to them with rapidity. He lifted his baton for the commencement of the downbeat, the orchestra looking at him with excited anticipation on their faces.

The music began to fill the theatre, and Alejandro played them, the musicians, as if extended from his arms, sweeping and cutting the air with his sea ivory. Violins and percussion resonated with delicate sprinklings of flute, oboe and clarinet, filling the hearts and souls of every person in the theatre, audience and players alike. The sounds encompassing the theatre were nothing less than pure, unadulterated magic.

With her cello clasped between her black-stockinged legs and the fiddle gingerly held in her right hand, Juanita watched Alejandro, mesmerized as he turned this way and that, smiling thinly then seriously as the score demanded. His entire body suffused the music, for he *was* the concerto. Juanita played with all the passion she could muster shining from her eyes. It was in the way she moved her arm as she played the fiddle against the strings of the instrument between her legs. Suddenly her eyes glazed, and she licked her lips sensuously. This was not possible! Oh no, not possible at all! Her arms became slack, her body rigid with ultimate, undeniable passion. This could not possibly be happening to her. He would kill her for ruining his performance on a public stage instead of his sumptuous bed.

A smile appeared on her attractive face as she bent slightly forward so that her long blonde hair fell over her face, concealing her orgasmic smile and erotic passion.

When Alejandro looked at the young woman for an instant, his baton urging her to play the passage at adagio while so enraptured in her own thoughts, the string section abruptly and incandescently switched to allegro, urged by her compelling performance, thereby committing the amazing *faux pas* of not being led by the conductor, if only for a brevity. She smiled with her eyes almost closed, and, for a moment, the maestro hesitated as he recognized the often-witnessed expression on her face. Only a maestro could carry on playing and not miss a beat at what was so obviously happening, at least to his private understanding, there on the stage. Fortunately, the string section quickly realized the error and compensated.

When the crescendo of the last notes ended with a final sweep of Alejandro's arms, the maestro bowed and left the stage stiffly and in a hurry, then returned to accept the applause from the audience shouting their bravos and encores. He briefly returned one more time, smiling at the crowd who exploded in wild exuberance

He also held out his hand to the young cellist, and Juanita paled, knowing she could not refuse. She got up from her chair somewhat awkwardly and approached him, nearing the great Alejandro Mañues. Together they took a bow towards the audience. He led her off stage with alacrity as the crowd exited for intermission. The orchestra manager overheard a partial statement before the maestro's door was slammed forcefully in his face. "You unseemly bitch! How could you do such an embarrassing—"

Later, when the second part of the program was about to begin, a tall, brown-haired woman occupied the chair where Juanita sat. Alejandro also seemed different, almost as though he had suffered a traumatic experience during the interim. The remaining performance proceeded without a hitch, much to everyone's satisfaction.

Everybody waited for the morning newspapers to appear with reviews of the opening performance.

Maria Lopez was revered for her critiques of cultural events in Buenos Aires. She wrote: "Was it the great Arturo Toscanini who once said, 'Madam, there you sit with that magnificent instrument between your legs, and all you can do is *scratch* it!' And let us not forget our own former maestro, Senor Villa-Lobos, who is reputed to have said to a disappointing performance of another female cellist, 'Madame, you can surely pluck your G-string, but I do not qualify that as music.' This said, our first cellist, whom I thought gave an extraordinary performance in the first half, was for some inexplicable reason replaced in the second. I am told it is indeed fortunate she was wearing a black dress, but do not clearly comprehend the remark. There is a rumour that our maestro may have been involved with a young woman resembling the lady, and if true, and they had a falling out during intermission, might explain the odd incident."

THE SNOOPER AND THE SOUTH END SNITCH

Betty Dobson

Halifax isn't like it used to be. Prostitution's the biggest business in the city; the Blowjobs practically own the South End. Murder runs a close second. Burglaries and assaults are up, too, more every year. Hell, if it's illegal, it's thriving. Some folks blame it on amalgamation, others on the casino. Who knew that either one of them would last this long?

The law still can't keep up with all the shit that's going down. Maybe the crooks are getting smarter. Personally, I think technology just makes them look that way. Least ways, I owe my livelihood to the current state of affairs.

My name's Bill Francis. I'm what's known in the trade as a Snooper. Let the Surfers do all their investigating online; I like to get my hands dirty now and then. Course, one of these days, they might not come clean.

My day normally starts around Noon. Today, it's almost two o'clock when I pull up to my office building. Not hard to tell that something's wrong. The cops have the street roped off, and five squad cars form a barrier between me and my office. I don't like trouble. Makes me nervous. When I get nervous, people get hurt.

Here comes Sgt. Dave Pomeroy, full of fire and brimstone—and probably three bowls of stew and half a loaf of bread. To say that Pomeroy has a hearty appetite is like saying Baryshnikov is a pretty good dancer. "Jesus, Francis," he says. "Where you been? We've been trying to reach you for hours. Get a cell phone, why don't you."

"What's going on, Pomeroy? Another bomb threat?"

Pomeroy shakes his head like a wet dog. "Nah, we ain't had one in over a week. You know a Frank Taylor?"

"Sure," I say. "I did some work for him last year."

"Yeah, well, looks like he killed his wife last night. Tried to make it look like a robbery. Been holed up in your office since mid-morning. Says he'll only talk to you,

and he'll shoot your secretary if we make a move on him."
Dave scratches his armpit and burps. "When'd you get a
new girl?"

"Last month. What kind of odds are you giving?"

"Only five-to-one on shooting the secretary, but it's
two-to-one he killed his wife."

"You got a witness?"

"Anonymous. Called in about three a.m., said she
heard two shots and saw Taylor's car drive away from the
house."

"Did you get a trace on her signal?"

"Nah, she used one of those old-style pay phones. Call
must've come from the South End, but the Blowjobs
aren't talking."

"Wouldn't be polite."

Pomeroy snorted. "Good one."

"Right. You want me to go in?"

"Only if you're wired. See if you can get him to
confess."

"I'll do it, but I have to be honest. I don't think Taylor's
guilty. He's not the type."

Pomeroy looks me square in the eye; I feel like a meaty
bone in an open garbage can. "Anybody can be the type,
Francis. Just depends on the situation. 'Sides, from what
I hear, Phoebe Taylor could drive anyone to murder."

My office is on the fifth floor. Any other day, I'd take
the stairs, but this feels like an elevator day. When I
reach my office, I notice the door is open. My secretary,
Sam, is lounging on the couch, smoking a cigarette.
There's no sign of Taylor. I catch Sam's eye, hunch my
shoulders, and throw up my hands to each side of my
head. *Where is he?*

She points her cigarette in the direction of the
bathroom door.

I motion for her to leave, but she shakes her head. The
bathroom door clicks open, so I step back against the wall
to keep myself concealed. Shuffling footsteps mark

Taylor's progress from the bathroom to the couch.

"Where is he?" That nasally voice can only belong to Taylor.

"Look," Sam says, "I already told you. I—don't—know. He's usually here by now." Silence. "Your fly's down."

Taylor squeaks once then starts grumbling. "It's stuck."

"Well, don't look at me."

I step into the office and quietly close the door behind me. Taylor's too busy fumbling with his zipper to notice me at first. I take a couple steps forward and clear my throat. "Need a hand with that, Frank?"

Taylor's head snaps up. He smiles at me like I'm his long-lost brother or something. "Bill! Thank God you're here. I'm in big trouble."

"Yeah, I heard. Threatening to kill Sam won't make things any better."

"Oh that. I never intended to hurt her. Man, I don't even have a gun."

"It's true, boss." Sam yawns. "He's been a perfect gentleman." Her cigarette gone, she starts chewing on a strand of her dark hair. She rubs her legs together so I'll notice the black lace cat suit she's wearing under her dress.

"Can you help me, Bill?"

Frank's whining brings me back to reality. "Okay, pal, tell me the truth. Did you kill Phoebe?"

"Only in my dreams. I never should have married her. She just wanted my money." Frank deflates into a chair and shakes his head. "It's not easy to admit, but . . . the only time she let me, you know, touch her was on the wedding night. She couldn't even pretend for the whole honeymoon."

I sit down across from him and lean forward. "Why didn't you just divorce her?"

"Sounds stupid now, but I really was in love with her. I thought if I was patient, she'd come around."

"Excuse me," Sam says as she pushes herself off the

couch. "Fascinating as this story is, I've heard it all before." She leans over me, revealing a hint of cleavage and more of the cat suit. "I got work to do. Can I use your computer?"

I reach into my coat pocket and pull out the key to my private office. My eyes are still locked on the black lace.

She takes the key with a perky "thank you" and slides into my office without another word.

Taylor watches her with obvious appreciation. "Wow. Where'd you find her?"

"Used to be my South End snitch. Took a chance and sent her to school. Turns out she's a whiz with computers."

"Damn it, Bill," Sam yells. "When's the last time you dusted this thing off?"

"Lucky for you," Taylor says.

"Yeah, well, she's been paying me back. With interest, if you know what I mean."

Taylor blushes a little at the suggestion but smiles anyway.

"Have you got an alibi?"

"Nothing I can prove. I was working late, getting ready for tax time. Profits are way down again."

"You still think someone's fudging the numbers?"

Taylor nods. "It doesn't seem so important right now. I just want to find out who killed her."

"You'd be better off turning yourself in."

"But . . ."

"You've done enough damage already. Taking a hostage makes you look guilty." Taylor starts to speak, but I cut him off. "Cut your losses, Frank."

Taylor chews his moustache for a few seconds. "You'll take my case?"

"Of course. I owe it to you for coming up empty last year."

"Bill," Sam yells again. "I need your password."

"Hold on. I'm coming." Taylor's looking a little jumpy, so I play it safe. "Frank, I'm gonna be straight with you.

I'm wearing a wire."

Taylor jumps up, knocking over the chair.

"Relax. You haven't said anything incriminating. I'm telling them they can come get you now. Hear that, Pomeroy? He's not armed, so go easy on him."

Once Taylor's gone, I disconnect the wire and head for the office.

Sam looks up from the computer with a frown. "This'd be a lot easier if you'd just tell me the password."

I join her behind the desk and point to the screen. "See here. It says 'Secret Password.' As in 'tell no one.' Push over."

She wheels away, sticking out her tongue in defiance. Then she licks her lips and blows me a kiss.

Scowling, I point my finger at her. "Keep it up, sweetness, and I'll send you back to the South End. Now turn around. I don't want you peeking." For a minute, I think she's actually going to keep quiet.

"Bad enough I had to go down there last night. Don't want anyone thinking I'm back on the market."

I don't even bother looking at her. "Quit complaining. That call was worth more than a lifetime spent on your back."

The cursor's blinking away in the centre of the screen, begging for my attention. Just takes one word to keep it happy right now. I type in "spennnn"—whoa, back up there, that should be "spenser"—and hit Enter. Keyboard's sticking a little today. That's what I get for buying second hand. And maybe Sam was right about dusting it once in awhile.

The screen blurs for a few seconds then a picture starts to take shape. It looks just like my office, except for the images of filing cabinets that don't exist outside the Net. Technology does have its uses.

"Can I come play now?" Not waiting for an answer, Sam hikes her dress and straddles my lap. Nuzzling my ear, she whispers, "Come on, Snooper. Let's play."

"You've got work to do. Remember?"

"That shit's boring. You said you'd show me the protected files someday."

"And someday I will."

"Oh come on," she says, sliding up and down. "Just give me the password to one of them."

"They're all the same, sweetness." I try to ignore her but can't help noticing the way her leg muscles move beneath the black lace.

Sam clasps her hands around my neck and leans back. "Really? That's kind of dumb, isn't it? Only thing dumber would be if they're the same as your main password."

Grabbing her wrists, I loosen her hands and lower her to the floor. "So I'm dumb. Too many passwords and I'd have to write them down. How secure would that be?"

Sam's not saying anything. She doesn't have to. I know that look in her eyes. Turning off the computer, I fall on top of her and collect some more interest on her "student loan."

The cops come back while Sam's off getting supper. Pomeroy and two of his men stroll into my office without knocking.

"Francis. Hard at work, I see."

"What's the matter, Pomeroy? Forget your toy?" I toss the wire to him. "Piece of junk's not worth keeping, anyway."

Pomeroy burps and motions his men forward. They take up positions on each side of me as Pomeroy pulls a card from his pocket. "William Eugene Francis, you are under arrest for the murder of Phoebe Taylor. Anything you say—"

"Cut the crap."

"Are you waiving the reading of your rights?"

"Sure as shit. What's going on, Pomeroy?"

He leans over the desk, giving me a good whiff of his most recent dining experience. "We've got evidence linking you to the Taylor murder. You're gonna want to call your lawyer." Glancing down, he smirks. "You might want to zip up while you're at it."

"I didn't even know Phoebe Taylor. What makes you think . . ." Then I remember Sam's curiosity about my password and the sticking keys on my keyboard. A snitch and a computer tap. They weren't taking any chances.

"It's all on your Net account, Francis, and now it's a matter of public record. That includes your 'entertainment' files. Blackmail's one thing, but did you have to bonk her? Did she know you got it all on video? Nice angles, by the way, but a little grainy. How much did that cost her?"

I lean back in the chair, out of range of the garlic. "Where's Sam?"

"Protective custody. We're letting her burn her episodes. Just our way of saying thanks." Pomeroy holds up the pieces of my discarded wire. "And this piece of junk, as you put it, is strictly hi-tech. Nanites. You could pulverize it under your heel, and it'd still broadcast all the way to Boston and back. But lucky you, they give free tech courses in prison. Might come in handy . . . if you ever get out."

NAMES
Phoebe Wray

She slashed his throat with a piece of the broken mirror. It satisfied—the faint wet bubble before the blood spurted and the bigger bubbles later.

"Die, my friend," she whispered.

He did.

"Ah, Esme, Esme," she crooned to herself, each "me" a kiss, "you are a baaaad girl." And she snickered and licked the blood that had splashed on her white hand. Salty. Fresh. Refreshing.

She had targeted him at the Stamford commuter rail station two weeks before, on an early Monday morning. He was rushing to make the train to Grand Central, still a little crusty around the edges of his sleepy brown eyes. His conservative tie was loose, suit jacket unbuttoned. He struggled to get on the train—balancing briefcase, thick, half-read paperback, folded morning paper, and a cup of coffee.

She laughed softly as she approached him. "Can I help? I'll take your coffee."

He gave her a grateful smile, let her take the cup, and nodded her onto the high step ahead of him.

She sat near a window. He appeared, still smiling and juggling items, to her left. "May I join you?"

"Please."

There was a problem with the coffee again as the train began to move. She reached for it. "Give me the coffee. But if I have to hold it a third time, I'll drink it."

That charmed him. He ensconced himself next to her with messy inefficiency and got his cup back.

He neglected the news and his paperback novel to talk. He was a good talker, moving quickly from the weather to the news of the day. He said nothing about television or sports.

"Do you live in Stamford?"

She shook her head, letting the long blond curls swish forward. "No. Just visiting a friend. I live in Chelsea."

"Were you in the city on 9/11?"

"No." And her eyes became grave and serious. "I was in L.A. on business." He couldn't know that was a lie; she didn't remember where she had been. "Were you? It must have been terrible."

"We had to run for it."

He talked modestly of himself, briefly describing his job on Wall Street. She made him laugh with stories about her position as a librarian for a midtown law firm. She had never been a librarian. Every man she found and marked and tested got a different story. That kept life interesting.

Sometimes she imagined she had been all those things—broker, salesclerk, boutique manager, real estate salesperson. (She always unsexed her language in the old-fashioned sixties way and listened carefully to discover if the man did, too. It was one of her signs.)

She didn't remember exactly when it had started, the need to test, the need to be someone other than who she was, the need to stop the pain with pain. She didn't remember who she was, except she harboured a vague image of her mother and father leaning over her, looking down with sharp eyes and teeth that resembled the picture of the wolf in her storybook. No matter. They were gone shortly after that.

The commuter from Stamford passed the first test, and the rest was easy. Meeting for a drink after "work." Riding back to the suburbs on the same train once again, of course, she said, to "visit her friend." They met mid-week for an early dinner, and he caught a late train.

It took only two weeks until he had wanted to see her in a more meaningful way, and on a weekend. He broached it as they left a movie theatre.

"Can we do this more often? I want to get to know you better. I'd like to see more of you, Esme."

She pretended melodramatic innocence. "More of me?

Just how to do mean that, sir?"

"Oh, c'mon," he chided, with the boyish way he had. "You know what I mean. I like you. I want more of you."

She offered her place in the city.

She gave him another hoop to jump through and suggested they go to a concert. Concerts were civilized, civilizing events. (Behind her hazel eyes was the memory of a violinist on a small stage, wiping his face with a handkerchief, she in the audience, chilled with beauty and weeping.) He agreed with only a twitch of his lips and didn't make a joke or say anything disparaging about classical music. He passed.

She insisted that they dress formally. "Part of the charm of it," she had breathed on him, her face close to his as they waited for the light to change at a busy street corner.

He nodded, his eyes drinking in her face, shifting his briefcase from hand to hand so he could push back a wispy strand of blond highlighted hair that the wind blew in her eyes. "A concert would be great. And some Esme after concert would be greater."

He had performed well and deserved his reward.

Simple to arrange the sacrifice. The delicious kill. A drink at a fake London-style pub, a short walk to a restored brownstone condo, the owner of which had vanished without a trace or a note the previous month. No one had missed him. At least, no messages clogged his answering machine. She had marked all his bills "deceased." She would be long gone before the bank or the landlord inquired. She had put his keys on a new fancy ring; the old leather one had been too blood stained to clean.

Now she brushed the glittering shards from her long blue dress, feeling the delicious pricks of glass stuck in the fabric, then crunched to the window through the remains of the mirror. The view was of a scraggly little vacant lot, dark now, the path that snaked through black lumps of trash faintly visible in light from a street lamp.

"Where are stray dogs when you need them?" She would invite them up for a snack, maybe. If they behaved themselves. If they didn't jump on her in gratitude. Stains are difficult to remove from metallic cloth. Harder than from pigskin. There never were dogs, but she liked to dream of it, of the exotic primitive feast that could occur, that she could watch and admire, maybe even learn something from.

She raised her arm languidly, watching its progress in the murky light, regretting—slightly—the broken mirror. It would have been pleasant to see herself reflected in a shaft of moonlight, the beauty of her arm encased in electric blue.

She danced then, humming, partnering herself from one window to the other, with tricky turns in between. She watched her body shimmer in the cold moonlight. "Esme, -me, -me, -me," she sang, "you should be on the Broadway stage!"

She whirled and then froze, catching her breath, imagining the sounds of pursuit.

"They're coming!" She gritted her teeth. She pretended, panted, listening to her heartbeat, pulling her shoulders up high, manufacturing panic. It felt good. Her thighs tingled. She bunched her toes cruelly in spike heels. Pain was good. She loved to be scared. It made her juices run.

She surveyed the messy room. He had not put up much of a fight, but he had tried to stop her from clearing everything off the tables with a swipe of her long fingers— he lurching awkwardly for the lamp as it teetered on the edge of the mahogany dresser. He had been an arguer. She didn't care for that type. (A flash memory of someone shouting at her to stop crying. Pain.)

Then, she had paused briefly in front of the mirror as if to adjust her hair. She watched his reflection as he picked up small fallen things—an ashtray, two magazines, a wine glass, a framed picture of an older couple. Parents, she guessed. She had smiled, wondering briefly who they were. (Wolf's teeth.)

Then his tall figure had loomed behind her as he put his arms around her waist, pulled her to him. He said soothing words into the nape of her neck, to manipulate her anger, but she could see white all around the pupils of his eyes. Stupid. He had shown fear.

That had done it. He was a cornered animal, but he was not willing to fight like one. She pulled the mirror from the wall and hit him over the head with it, shattering their images into pieces, the way her own life had been shattered so long ago when she had found the still hot heart of love and pain. Then she had played with the long silvery shards until he was dead and she was fulfilled.

Now, she smoothed the waterfall of the blue dress over slim hips, her hands moving upward to cup her breasts and squeeze. She felt good. Peaceful. She conjured her past accomplishments.

"I am Angel, with the sweet smile; shy Brigid; Cassandra, who always wore red; Delores, who danced; and Esme, of the brilliant mind." She deliberately sought the largest shiny chunks on the floor, obliterating the faint reflection of the ceiling with each name, the heels of her blue pumps grinding until the mirror was dust.

"So many sinners; so little time." And she laughed a musical laugh, touching her breasts again. "What next? Hmmm.

"What does this mean? This death? This joy?" Her voice was a dramatically harsh whisper. She waited for answer from the Cosmos, expecting none. She giggled.

She always asked the questions, a part of her ritual. It made her feel powerful to know there was no reason in what she did, and no pattern, except for the names, and only she knew about that.

She glanced around the ruined, darkened room. Her eyes never found his sprawled body. "This is the meaning of my existence. I am who I say I am! And who am I to be now? Francine? Flora? No—something strong and butch . . . Frieda! Ja! Germanic. Nazi! I will kill like a Nazi. I look smashing in black and silver."

Good, she thought, *that's settled.* She wanted a drink.

Suddenly, a shadow crossed the window. Was that the fire escape? She couldn't remember. The brief, dark image had looked like a person.

"I am Frieda! Strong. Fearless. Deadly! Who dares interrupt me?" She fancied Nazis spoke in clipped short sentences.

Her breasts thrust out, her back straightened, her knees locked, and she marched herself to the nearest of two windows. She dared instantly to thrust her head through its open pane and look around. Yes, there was a fire escape. No, there was no one there. She turned away and wheeled back, the hairs on the back of her neck rising unexpectedly. Fright. Her instinct was flight. Her response was to stick her head out again, ecstatic in her fear.

A tall woman stood on the fire escape in a long white gown. It seemed to be made of gauze. It covered her body but revealed everything—the long shapely legs, curving hips, high-riding breasts. The dress billowed in the slight wind theatrically, beautifully.

"I am Frieda the Nazi," she whispered to herself. To the woman in gauze she barked, "Who are you?"

There was no answer, and the form got fuzzy in her killer eyes, fuzzy, and—desirable. She tried a cruel smile. "I am Frieda. You are beautiful. Come. Let me make you welcome."

The lovely woman in the transparent dress stepped through the window, soundless and ephemeral as a wraith. Frieda moved back to allow egress, bowing smartly, stiffly, watching the other woman glide across the moon-swept room.

Frieda clenched her teeth, regretting that she was not yet in the costume: the black and silver with a death's head emblem. That was a bother. It was not proper. "You must tell me who you are!" she demanded, pleased that at least her accent was good.

The other woman surveyed the room calmly, ignoring

the question, glanced at the body sprawled in the glittering mirror-dust. She approached the man and stooped to touch his face then turned as she rose.

It was one smooth, graceful movement. The stiletto-length shard of mirror in her upraised hand caught the whole image of the moon before it sliced across the long, beautiful neck of Angel and Esme and Frieda.

"You have met Zelda," she whispered and smiled as she watched the body fall.

AUTHOR BIOS

Betty Dobson is an award-winning creative writer whose work has appeared in *Apollo's Lyre, Brady Magazine, Eros & Rust, Jerry Jazz Musician, Sol Magazine,* and *Toasted Cheese,* as well as in several anthologies and through the Amazon Shorts program. She released her first poetry collection, *Paper Wings,* in 2006 and is hard at work on her first short fiction collection. She is also the owner of InkSpotter Publishing, a partner in Done East Productions, the Editor of *Poetry Canada* magazine, the Networking Editor with *WE Magazine for Women,* and the Contributing Poetry Editor with *Apollo's Lyre.* Her personal website is www.bettydobson.ca.

James Dorr's new book, *Darker Loves: Tales of Mystery and Regret,* was released in December 2007 by Dark Regions Press as a companion to his previous collection, *Strange Mistresses: Tales of Wonder and Romance* (Dark Regions, 2001). Other work has appeared in such venues as *Alfred Hitchcock's Mystery Magazine, New Mystery, Aboriginal SF, Fantastic Stories, Future Orbits, Shadows of Saturn, Gothic.net, Chi-Zine, Dark Wisdom, Enigmatic Tales* (UK), *Faeries* (France), and numerous anthologies. Dorr is an active member of SFWA and HWA, an Anthony (mystery) and Darrell (fiction set in the US mid-South) finalist, a Pushcart Prize nominee, and a multi-time listee in *The Year's Best Fantasy and Horror.* He resides in the midwestern United States with a large, grey-and-black cat named Wednesday whose favourite toys are her collection of plastic spiders.

Krys Douglas teaches Humanities, Religion, Theatre, and Cultural Studies at Central New Mexico Community College. She won a fifth grade prize for a poem she wrote and has been writing ever since. She has published numerous academic articles and several short stories and poems. She is currently at work on a novel about medieval Iceland.

Everett Gavel is a freelance writer, editor, and poet who can be found at www.everettgavel.com. His favourite part of life is being "Daddy" to his daughters. He works in the Assistive Technology field, helping blind and low-vision computer users achieve success, while also working to make the World (Wide Web) a more accessible place.

Quitting the teaching rat race after twenty-two years, **Gary R. Hoffman** now lives in a motor home, travels the North American continent, and says, "Home is where you park it!" He has published over 200 short stories and has won or placed in many contests for short stories. Visit him at www.garyrhoffman.com.

Gail Kavanagh is a freelance writer living in Queensland, Australia. Gail has been published in anthologies and print and online publications. She is the author of several books, including *The Working Writer's Market Guide*.

Gail A. Laursen, raised nomadically in communities throughout British Columbia and Manitoba, now lives in Vulcan, Alberta. A graduate of Northwest Community College, Gail spent thirteen years in corporate accounting before pursuing her passion to write. While living in Drumheller, Alberta, she enjoyed experience as staff reporter for *The Valley Times* and became moderator for an online writers' group. With diverse reading interests, Gail also delights in outdoor photography, sewing, painting, and gourmet cooking, but is presently focusing on the crafting of her first novel, a Neolithic coming-of-age quest.

Brenda Roberts is married and lives with her husband of nearly twenty years in Fort Worth, Texas. She writes fantasy, fiction, poetry, and essays, and loves to read the same.

Gretchen Wilsenach is South African. Right after high school, she attended art college and obtained a Diplôme de Langue (in French). She managed an animation studio, had a career in advertising as television and radio producer for twenty years, and was a director/shareholder of a leading advertising agency. She travelled extensively through the years 1972 to 2008. She is currently organizing exclusive tours to Morocco. Gretchen is the author of *The Midnight Room*, a first novel. A second novel, *The Agreement*, is ready for publishing. She is the travel editor for *Dossier Magazine* in South Africa. Her hobbies include reading, movies, music (any genre as long as it is good), cooking creative, exotic dishes . . .and travelling! Next destination, India!

Diana Woods (http://web.mac.com/dianawoods) lives in Los Angeles and has been employed as a licensed clinical social worker in mental hospitals and clinics for over thirty years. She began participating in online writers' workshops in 2000 and started sending her work out in 2005. Currently she's enrolled in Internet classes at the UCLA Writer's Workshop. Her work has been published in Web journals and small print publications including: *The Hiss Quarterly, Flashquake, Riverbabble, Doorknobs and Body Paint, Salome,* and *Flash Me Magazine.*

Phoebe Wray is a long-time non-fiction writer, playwright and poet who has begun to publish in the spec-fic field. Her futurist action-adventure novel, *JEMMA 7729*, was released in March 2008 by EDGE Science Fiction and Fantasy Publishing. She's had stories in *Andromeda Spaceways Inflight Magazine, Farthing, Fables.org, Chi-Zine, Faerie Nation Mag, PanGaia,* and *SageWoman.* She's on the Motherboard of Broad Universe and lives in a small town outside of Boston with three cats and a houseful of books.

AUTHOR INDEX

www.ingramcontent.com/pod-product-compliance
Lightning Source LLC
Chambersburg PA
CBHW072005170626
46813CB00005B/2024